Silver Bells

The Shops on Wolf Creek Square

Gini Athey

Editing: Brittiany Koren
Cover art design/Layout: Ed Vincent/ENC Graphics
Cover Illustrations: Shutterstock.com
Map illustration by Logan Stefonek/Stefonek Illustration & Design

Category: Women's Fiction/Romance

First Print Edition November 2018.
0 1 2 3 4 5 6 7 8 9

Wolf Creek Square Series

Book 1 – Quilts Galore

Book 2 – Country Law

Book 3 – Rainbow Gardens

Book 4 – Square Spirits

Book 5 – BookMarks

Book 6 – Town Hall

Dedication

*To Lloyd F. —a very special friend,
who kept pestering me about Marianna and
Art's relationship as each book in
the series was released.*

Dear Readers,

Silver Bells is a surprise, even to me. When I outlined the six books for my series, *The Shops on Wolf Creek Square*, I never thought about adding a novella as a bonus story. But things change. As each book was released, I'd receive emails asking about the relationship between Marianna Spencer and Art Carlson, which began at the end of Book 1, *Quilts Galore*. In subsequent books, they appeared together and were obviously a couple, but still coping with not-quite-adult kids. Readers weren't satisfied with simply noticing Art and Marianna having pie and coffee at Crossroads or showing up together at Square events. Readers—and Art and Marianna, themselves—kept nagging me. When were these two going to have their day?

As it turns out, Marianna and Art have managed to keep their two-year engagement a secret, but time passes, children grow up, and they're finally free to make their own plans. Everyone on the Square is thrilled about their wedding. Marianna is excited about her small, but joyful and elegant post-Christmas wedding. Odd, though, one hitch in the plans after another interferes with what Marianna wants.

With the holiday shopping rush at hand, Marianna has little time to fret and no one else has time to sympathize. As the day approaches, Marianna is forced to accept that even her wedding isn't going to be anything like the dress she designed herself.

What's gone wrong? Then, in an instant, Marianna learns exactly why so much has gone awry.

Nestled in rich farm land, Wolf Creek is a small fictional town west of Green Bay, Wisconsin. Wolf Creek Square is a pedestrian-only area where historical buildings surround a courtyard. Concerts and festivals—and weddings—are held in the Square, now a four-season destination.

So come along to the gathering and meet again the men and women—and a few kids—you've enjoyed in the other books. If you haven't read all the books, that's okay. Chances are, you'll recognize them anyway, because all the residents of the Square show up in most all the books. As you'll see, many residents from the previous books (Book 1, *Quilts Galore;* Book 2, *Country Law*; Book 3, *Rainbow Gardens;* Book 4, *Square Spirits*; Book 5, *BookMarks; and* Book 6, *Town Hall*) are all part of this send off for Marianna and Art and the people of Wolf Creek Square.

So, thanks for going on this Wolf Creek Square journey with me. I hope you'll enjoy the bustle of activity on the Square and visit my website, www.giniathey.com to sign up for my newsletter. You never know what gossip you might hear.

Gini Athey
2018

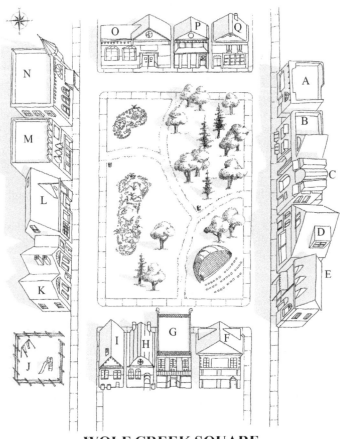

WOLF CREEK SQUARE

A-Farmer Foods
B-The Fiber Barn
C-Rainbow Gardens
D-Clayton's
E-Country Law
F-Art&Son Jewelry
G-Quilts Galore
H-The Toy Box
I-BookMarks

J-Fenced Playground
K-Heirlooms - Past and Future
L-Styles by Knight and Day
M-Biscuits and Brew
N-The Inn
O-Museum
P-Mayor's Office
Q-Square Spirits

*"Happy is the wife who finds a true friend,
and far happier is she who finds that
true friend in her husband."*
—*Unknown*

October
1

I sat on the bench in front of my shop on that warm October evening and waited for Art to arrive for what we'd long called our "bench dates." We'd had many of those dates over the last five years, mainly because those evenings gave us time together after our hectic days as shop owners on Wolf Creek Square. Art and his son, Alan, created unique pieces of jewelry in their shop, Art&Son, next door to my quilt shop, Quilts Galore. Both shops were located on the west end of the Square. I lived upstairs with my stepdaughter, Rachel and her son, Thomas. Quiet times were rare at work or at home.

As always, my heart fluttered when I saw Art approaching. A free-spirit, for sure, Art was also blessed with a calm nature that appealed to me as much as his strong, tenor voice. He tilted my world and had from the first time I'd met him on the day I bought the quilt shop. Now he took a few steps more and bent forward to put his hands on the back of the bench, encasing me in his arms.

I'd waited all day for the kiss that would come. I wasn't disappointed. "Can I ask for more?"

"I'll give you a thousand more, if that's what you want, Marianna." The second kiss spoke of passion.

"Is there a limit?" I asked.

He sat next to me and took my hand to rest between his. "Infinity."

We'd bantered about our special kisses many times and always ended on a note that meant forever.

"Isn't it beautiful tonight?" I couldn't hide my smile. I was savoring an idea I'd share with him. But I didn't want to rush, so instead I chatted about the string of warm days we'd had. I commented on the colorful leaves in the courtyard in front of us and the way the light breeze formed mini-tornadoes that sent the leaves dancing across the grass. Pumpkins and mums and smiley-faced scarecrows dotted the walkway. Fairy lights shaped like pumpkins hung in the mostly leafless trees creating an orange glow over the courtyard. "I'm always amazed that the decorations and lights appear overnight and I never hear the trucks."

"I suspect they have good gremlins helping them. We don't have those extra pairs of hands showing up in our stores, so we try to do too much by ourselves." Art rested against the back of the bench.

I squeezed his hand. "I wouldn't have it any other way. Would you?"

"Nah, not really. So what kind of Halloween decorations are you planning for this year?"

I twisted to look over my shoulder at the front window of my shop. The Labor Day and back-to-school themes looked dated, which they were. "Honestly, I haven't thought about it. Maybe I'll make a scarecrow, if you or Alan will share a shirt and jeans. I could put together a child-size one using some clothes Thomas has outgrown, and I have a pumpkin quilt I can use as a backdrop. And you?"

Art shook his head. "Nothing that elaborate. Just a couple of Megan's hand-carved pumpkins, which I need to order now. I like to keep the display cases clear. Better to make the jewelry show." Always the salesman, Art never wanted elaborate decorations to overshadow his brooches and rings.

"Maybe you'd like to use this Art&Son blue box for your display." I pulled my surprise out of my coat pocket. It was the box Art had given me two years ago. A smile spread across my face. "Way back then you said when the right time comes, you want to marry me."

Art paused. Staring at the box, he didn't take a breath. "Now?"

"Yes," I whispered. "I don't want to wait any longer. We've been keeping our engagement secret for two years. It's been hard. I can't tell you how many times I've wanted to blurt out our news."

Still waiting for a response, I pulled my hand from his and cradled his face. "I love you, Art. I have for years. You know that. But with Rachel and Thomas living with me and Alan with you, it was always the wrong time for us. Now, with the kids engaged and planning their future, *we* can be together."

Smiling, Art took the ring from the box and slipped it on my finger. "And here I thought after so long you might have changed your mind."

I heard the teasing in his voice, but I wasn't being lighthearted when I whispered, "Never."

Art stood up and pulled me into his arms and twirled me around like we were kids. "Okay, it's time to celebrate with coffee and pie." He planted a quick kiss on my lips, but three more times we slowed our trip to Crossroads, the restaurant across the Square from our shops, so we could indulge in kisses that said more than words.

Finally arriving, the hostess escorted us to "our" table, the one we occupied most evenings. Oh, we would take another table if guests sat there, but those evenings never seemed to be as enjoyable. That night, though, only the table that was a special part of our world would do.

I looked around the familiar room. "I bet Cameron will upgrade the dining room now that he owns The Inn."

My observation went unnoted because the waitress stopped to fill our water glasses and take our order. Art and I decided we needed chocolate mousse pie—a legendary Crossroads' offering—and coffee. I wish I'd kept a record of the number of times we'd ordered that same dessert over the last five years.

Art moved the small vase of fresh flowers that was in the middle of the table. "You'd think they would set these off to the side."

"They're called *center*…pieces, Art." I laughed at his mock pouty face. We'd had this conversation more than a few times.

"Center, or not, it's annoying to look through them. I'd rather look at you."

The waitress bro The first bite of the cold pie was always a delight. The smooth texture of the mousse and the dark rich color all added to the special flavor.

I couldn't take my eyes off my ring. Not a traditional style, Art had surprised me by using the logo from my shop, the nine-patch quilt square as the design. Set on point, each of the small outside squares was a different gem stone in my favorite jewel-tone colors. A diamond, shining clear and bright from the spotlight above the table, was nestled in the middle square. I loved it, as I loved the man who'd made it. Someday, I would tell him how many times I'd taken the ring and put it on my finger and spun my dreams about the life we'd have one day.

I looked at him and tried to put into words what he meant to me, but Art looked beyond my shoulder, toward the front of the restaurant.

"Well, look who's stopping by to say hello."

I twisted in my chair to see Jack and Liz approaching. A jolt of excitement traveled through me. Liz had been my best friend for a long time, many years before I left Green Bay and moved to Wolf Creek. I'd managed to keep my secret from her, so I was excited to finally share the news.

When William, my first husband was alive, we'd been backyard neighbors to Liz and Jack, and they had been with us through William's bout with pancreatic cancer from the earliest doctor's appointments through the last week as he slipped away. I'd lost my life partner, and Jack had lost his best friend. My move to Wolf Creek Square had strained our relationship until Jack's heart attack prompted their move to Wolf Creek so Jack could work in a less stressful law office.

Jack leaned on the back of a chair. "We were hoping to get here earlier, but Liz had a conference call with Matt and Sarah about the books. Liz is doing a huge share of the work getting Sarah's town history into book form for the holidays."

"No problem," Art said. "We're not ready to leave yet, so join us." Art rose to pull out a chair for Liz.

Always on the excitable side, Liz gasped as she was about to sit. I might have known. Liz never missed a beat—she had a knack for sensing change and her powers of observation were unmatched. She stared at my ring. "When? How? I want details."

Making her wait a few minutes longer, Art casually filled their cups with coffee from our carafe. "Marianna asked me to marry her. Just now." He made it sound like it was nothing special, just part of our evening's conversation.

"And you just happened to have this unique ring ready?" Liz reached over and tapped the gem stones with her finger.

I spoiled his joke with my small burst of laughter. "Not really. Would you believe I've had the ring for two years?"

"*Two years*? And you never told me?" Liz flopped back in her chair. "Have you forgotten I'm your best friend and I know everything about you? Or has that changed?" Her voice had a flustered edge to it.

"Easy, Liz," Jack said, frowning. "Give Marianna a chance to explain. But first, we'll order dessert and more coffee. This sounds too interesting to rush." He raised his hand to get the waitress' attention.

After they ordered their pie and carafe of decaf, Liz said, "Now, Marianna, spill."

I shrugged. Liz was smart enough to figure this out on her own, but she wanted to hear it all. "The time hasn't been right for us to get married, even though we knew we'd be together someday. Two years ago, Art gave me the ring to seal it, and we agreed it was *our* secret. We both had teenagers at home and Thomas was part of my life. Now the kids are engaged, so we have no reason to wait any longer."

I glanced across the table at Art and the rest of the room faded into the background. I knew when Liz thought about it, she'd realize sharing this secret only with Art was wonderfully romantic.

"So when's the...?" Liz was interrupted when the waitress arrived and emptied her tray of plates and coffee.

Art was in rare form with his claim that *I'd* asked *him* to marry me. "I agreed to this marriage only a couple of hours ago, so we haven't made any plans yet."

"Maybe you and Rachel should get married at the same time. You know, keep it a family affair." Liz's eyes sparkled with pride over her idea.

We'd given Liz a bone to chew on, and from past experience, I knew I would be bombarded with questions and suggestions for days to come. I imagined Rachel and Alan would prefer to make their own plans. Maybe Art and I would elope and surprise everyone.

Our conversation eventually pivoted to the surge of visitors the Square would see between Halloween and Christmas and a bit about the client base at Country Law. But whenever Liz saw an opening, our talk traveled back to the wedding. She was all about gathering Megan and Rachel for a women's night of brainstorming.

I laughed at most of her suggestions, honestly admitting I hadn't given any thought to dates or details about the wedding or what I'd wear, or even where it would be.

"We need to sit down with a calendar and…" she insisted.

The lights in the dining room dimmed. Oops, we'd closed Crossroads yet again. At least it saved me from giving her another "I don't know" answer. Liz wouldn't be the only person in our tight-knit community that would have questions about the when and where, and who would stand with us, and what I'd wear. All those details were too much, too soon for me.

Admittedly, the busiest time of the year on the Square was not the ideal time to plan a wedding. I wanted to marry Art and I wanted to share our day with friends. So what was one more item on my to-do list?

Jack and I made our way to the front of the restaurant. Liz had Art cornered and was asking more questions. "You shared wonderful news with us tonight. You know, I like Art." Jack laughed and shook his head. "Maybe not so much on poker night when he takes my money."

When Liz and Art joined us, Art held out his hand. "Enjoyed the evening, Jack. Let's have dinner soon, before the crazy holiday times begin."

"I'm all for that." Jack shook Art's hand and offered one more round of congratulations.

Liz gave Art a hug, and then pulled me into her arms. "Love you, my friend. See you at coffee."

"Our car is in the back lot, so we'll head out this way." Jack grabbed Liz's hand before she could ask either of us one more question.

I waved, and Art and I were on our way out the front door.

In the clear night sky, it seemed a thousand stars sparkled. The leaves on the ground were tossed about by a light breeze. The cooler air had me snuggling closer to Art as we made our way to the end of the Square.

"I enjoyed how you kept Liz waiting for answers. She always has to be the first to know the latest news," I said with a light chuckle.

"She kept asking questions right up to when Jack pulled her away. Good thing Jack is so laid back," Art said. "Those two balance each other, don't you think?"

"That's too philosophical for tonight." The orange pumpkin lights in the courtyard reminded me of the fire I'd been carrying for Art for years, so I made him think of me by pulling him into my arms and telling him I loved him.

"We should have married years ago." He held my face and awarded me with a dozen light kisses.

"We've covered that a million times. You know it would've been complicated." I looked toward our shops and saw lights on in both apartments. "See? The kids are waiting for us, just like we used to stay up until they got home."

"Any clue when they're getting married?" he asked.

"Not really. Rachel picked up information at the spring wedding show she worked with Megan, but she talks more about the fun she's having working with Gwen at The Inn and coordinating the various upcoming events there."

"Yeah, Alan is really quiet about their plans and vague anytime I ask a specific question."

We'd reached the steps to Quilts Galore. "If Rachel is still awake, I want to tell her our news. I think you should tell Alan tonight. They're our family and they should be the first to know, well, second now that we've talked to Jack and Liz."

"Then it's good night for us. And, thank you for asking me to marry you." He bent forward to give me a parting kiss. "I'm very happy to say yes."

I gave him a mocking pointed look, but when I looked into his eyes, all I found was love.

He waited for me to relock the door before waving and turning away.

I didn't linger in the shop as I might have done on another night when my thoughts were racing and I needed to think. Tonight was about action. I climbed the steps to my home—our home—Rachel's, Thomas' and mine, calling, "Rachel? Are you up? I saw the light on."

She met me at the top of the stairs. "Hi. Something wrong?"

"Matter of fact, everything's right." I couldn't wait, so I boldly held out my left hand.

"Wow. Awesome. When?" After that, she seemed at a loss for words.

"Couple of hours ago. I asked him."

"Don't say another thing." She held out her hand to stop me. "This is so cool. We need wine and a full story."

She went into the kitchen and pulled out the formal wine glasses—goblets, really—while I went to the front window to gaze out at the Square. A few minutes later, we touched our glasses in congratulations. Quick to pick up the pile of bridal magazines from the love seat, she pulled my arm for me to sit. "Now, tell me more."

I rambled on about meeting Art the first day I bought the quilt shop and decided to move to Wolf Creek. She knew that, since she had moved with me. Some parts about Art and me falling in love were private, and I wouldn't tell anyone about my dreams for us or how fast our relationship developed.

I jumped to the night Art gave me the ring and how we'd agreed to marry when the time was right for all of us. In the meantime, we'd keep it our secret.

"Two years ago? You and Art have been engaged for *two years*? And you said nothing all this time?" Her voice echoed Liz's from earlier at Crossroads.

"Our romantic secret hasn't been hard to keep. Besides, everyone knows we've been seeing each other for years. Now with you and Alan engaged and getting ready to start your life together, Art and I can get on with ours."

"You and Art waited for Alan and me?" Tears pooled in her eyes. "For five years, you waited for *us* to grow up?"

Her depth of realization and understanding confirmed my belief that Rachel was worth all the bumps and troubles we'd traversed since she arrived at my doorstep, baby Thomas in her arms, no money, no food for her son, and quite literally, nothing more than the clothes she wore that day.

Rachel got up after swallowing the last drop in her glass. "I love you, Marianna. Thomas loves you, too, but forgets to say it." She leaned in for a hug. "Congratulations. Art is such a good man."

"Glad you think so," I chuckled.

"His son is good, too, so yes, I say so." She carried our glasses to the kitchen. "Take it from me, you'll get a million questions about your wedding plans."

"Art and I saw Jack and Liz at Crossroads tonight. She started in as soon as she noticed the ring."

She laughed. "Ha! Typical Liz. So, I guess I'll give you a day or two before I start asking for the details." She declared herself ready to sleep and lifted her hand in a goodnight wave as she headed down the short hallway to the room she shared with Thomas.

I wasn't ready to end the day. My mind kept meandering to the events that had brought me here. My husband, gone seven years now, had known Art from his frequent visits over the years to buy Art's brooches for me. He had given me so many that my jewelry box overflowed with the one-of-a-kind pieces. I wore a different one each day to cross-market for Art, but also because I loved every one of them.

It was one of Art's pieces that had brought me to Wolf Creek Square five years ago. The clasp on a Primrose flower brooch had broken and I wanted it repaired. It was the last piece William had given me before he died.

That same day, a For Sale sign in the quilt shop had stirred something in me, an awakening of sorts. I no longer wanted to be alone in my sewing room making quilts while surrounded by pieces of my life with William. I wanted to be part of a community that enjoyed life and worked hard to make their businesses successful. Five years later, I couldn't have asked for a richer life.

I slipped the ring from my finger and put it on my nightstand. I'd finally relaxed to a point where sleep would come quickly. I ran my finger over the stones one last time, smiling to myself. I'd wear my ring to morning coffee and watch as the news traveled to the other shopkeepers on Wolf Creek Square.

2

Art was on the bench waiting for me the next morning when I left Quilts Galore. He immediately took my hand and bent forward to kiss me. "It's legal now," he laughed.

"It was legal before, but I liked being private about our lives."

"True enough," Art said, grinning.

Biscuits and Brew—known as B and B—had become the gathering place for shopkeepers and employees in the morning before our shops opened at 10:00. The men always gathered at one table and the women at another, but we all shared selling strategies, discussed festivals, and the tour buses that brought so many of our shoppers.

Some of our friends had arrived earlier and were already enjoying their morning coffee. I immediately spotted Liz. When she saw the ring, she lifted an eyebrow and put her finger to her lips telling me my secret was safe with her.

The waitress placed a mug of my favorite blend in front of me. "Morning, Marianna."

"Thanks, Nancy. Great morning, huh?"

Sarah and Sadie had followed us in and slid into open chairs at the table. Sadie rarely came to coffee since she'd moved into the apartment above Heirlooms, but Sarah was a regular.

As was typical, Megan Reynolds bounced in with her smile as wide as her face. She sat in the empty chair next to me and put her notebook and tablet in the center of the table. "Going to be a busy week. Our first wedding in the new banquet room is this weekend. Lots to coordinate."

I watched her eyes get big when she saw my ring. "Don't tell me it's old news."

Sadie, never one to shy away from gossip, asked, "What news?"

Megan picked up my arm to show Sadie. "Marianna's ring."

The table erupted with questions when I told them I'd said yes to Art's proposal.

"Actually, she asked me," Art said from the next table. He tipped his chair on its back legs to be sure he was heard. The other men guffawed at the news, but quickly followed up with handshakes and back slapping.

Always ready for new clients, Megan offered her business, *Weddings at Wolf Creek Square,* if I needed help. "Would be a great testimonial if a shopkeeper on the Square used our services. But you need to pick a date soon, if you plan to use the banquet room."

"Art and I haven't talked about any plans yet," I said.

"Any date you choose is fine with me." Art's voice was loud enough for everyone to hear. "But let's keep it to this year."

I sent a text to Rachel asking for the date of an open Saturday evening in the banquet room before the end of the year.

She came back with, *Only 1 open, Saturday after Xmas.*

I replied, *Taken.*

I was saved from more unanswerable questions when Sarah's watch beeped. After resigning as the Square's manager and becoming a shopkeeper herself, I'd been surprised when she hadn't deleted the reminder beep. That day I was grateful for the familiar sound.

After returning to Quilts Galore, I looked over the shop and loosely planned for the holiday sales. October was a common deadline month for quilters making large Christmas gifts, quilts mostly. Smaller projects, like table runners or tree skirts could be put off until closer to the holiday.

The bell jingled, and I welcomed my first customer of the day.

Carla Barkley returned the greeting. I'd inherited the young-at-heart senior customer from Barbara Martin when I bought the shop. She came with a Halloween-themed tote bag on her arm.

"Looks like you're ready for Halloween," I said.

"Always like to show off my sewing." Carla held the bag for me to see the different spooky fabrics she'd used, including a glow-in-the-dark children's fabric I carried.

"I recognize some of those pieces. So what can I help you find today?"

"Well…um…you see. I know how busy this time of year can be for you and I was wondering if you could use some help." She worried the straps on her tote. "I mean, as an employee. You know, part-time."

That came as a surprise. "Well, I haven't given much thought about hiring anyone right now." The jingling bell and four women coming through the door distracted me. I didn't know what more I could say.

It gave Carla time to hand me a small paper with her name and phone number. "You're busy now. I can see that. But remember, I know fabric and quilting. I don't need a lot of training." She waved a good-bye.

No, she wouldn't, slipped through my mind. I mulled over Carla's idea, along with noting the changes going on with my usual holiday help. Rachel was working full-time as an event coordinator at The Inn and Liz was knee-deep in the production of Sarah's two-volume town history, a perfect match for her creative and technical skills.

The women scattered to different areas of the shop, so I went to offer my help to the nearest quilter and asked if she'd been to Quilts Galore before. I made no apology for not remembering every person that had visited my shop during the last five years.

"First trip, but I see it won't be my last. We're visiting family in Green Bay and the four of us are trying to get to as many quilt shops as we can while we're here."

"How fun." I began to straighten small cuts of fabric in a nearby basket, one of those forever jobs.

"We've noticed that some of the shops specialize in fabric

21

collections or reproduction colors or designs. Do you have a focal fabric?" she asked.

"Not really. I try to keep a little of a large assortment available. Many of my customers are visitors to the area, like you."

"What's keeping you, Theresa? Talking or buying today?" Her companion carried three bolts of green fabric when she joined us.

I was able to spend time with each quilter and by the time they left with fabric, books, and patterns, my shop needed an end-to-end straightening. I smiled because when my shop looked messy I'd made shoppers happy.

I'd only put one area in order when the bell announced my next customer, who brought a pattern and the fabric was easily cut. She, too, left with a smile on her face and a full Quilts Galore bag on her arm.

By mid-afternoon I hadn't had a break or a chance to text Art. That seemed to be the way we communicated most often. Customers were the name of the game and I'd had enough that day to put a smile on my face.

Art had an evening meeting with an engaged couple to design a set of matching wedding bands, so I ate a quick takeout dinner and readied the shop for the next day. Between thinking about the holidays and having a wedding to ponder, I went to bed tired and happy.

***

A week later, I called Carla. If I had no alternative plan, Rachel would make herself available on her days off from The Inn, but she had Thomas to consider. Rachel liked working and making money, but I needed someone who could be flexible. At one time Liz had worked for me, but she began her own business maintaining mailing lists and websites and social media for others on the Square.

Carla would be available when I needed her. The day after I offered her the job, she showed up ready to learn the business side of the shop. She had the energy and enthusiasm of a younger woman and knew the language of quilting as well as I did.

I realized my good fortune when she satisfied a difficult customer who wanted preferential treatment. I'd swallowed many words in the past trying to please that woman, but Carla spoke her language, and together they found the perfect fabric for her project.

A few days later, I was confident Carla could handle shoppers while I finished the window display. I'd gone with my original idea of two scarecrows and the pumpkin quilt, but it looked sparse with lots of open spaces. I tossed trick-or-treat candy on the floor to fill in the open areas, but that didn't help much. I asked Carla for her ideas.

"How about using my tote and some Halloween yardage? That would show the fabric you're actually selling. Correct?" With that, she turned to help a mother-daughter duo.

"Fabric, right," I said under my breath, my chuckle softening my words. It was so obvious I missed it. "You can keep your tote."

***

I was checking my new order list when I noticed "10 weeks" printed in small letters on a date on the calendar. Only one other person used that calendar as a schedule reminder. Rachel.

Was it a hint that I hadn't made any decisions about the wedding, other than securing a date and the banquet room at The Inn? Rachel had been tentative with her questions about my wedding plans, knowing I was getting bombarded with them already. She'd experienced the same questions after Alan had asked her to marry him at the 4th of July picnic. That made us kindred spirits, as the saying went.

I sent a text to Art asking if his evening was free. He replied with why? Embellished with a heart emoji.

Wedding plans, I sent back.

Right. C + D 7:30

I laughed at how quickly we'd learned the short cut language of texting. "Coffee and Dessert" had been reduced to C + D. To tell him I'd gotten his reply, I typed in two hearts.

***

That evening, we sat at our table at Crossroads and I began asking him his opinion on the twenty-five questions I'd copied from one of Rachel's bridal magazines. Why I thought I needed to do that was beyond me.

"Let's start with the invitation list." I took a swallow of coffee to give him time to consider the question.

"Just us." But his smile told me he was making light of the question.

"Not acceptable. Be serious." I put my pen down and took a bite of pie.

"If you insist. So, since neither of us has much in the way of family, I want everyone on the Square invited."

"Good. See? We agree on our guest list." I paused.

Art reached across the table for my hand. "Look, Marianna, you don't need my input or approval on any of these details. If I didn't trust your judgment, why would I marry you?"

"Because I make your heart sing?"

He laughed. "Well, there's that. So, okay, let's quickly finish your list." He refilled my cup with the last from the carafe.

"I'm glad you trust me, but we need to share some of this—it's a lot of work, and I don't want to make all the decisions myself." I scanned my notes. "So, who's your best man?"

"Alan, of course. I'll ask him soon. And for you?"

"I've seesawed back and forth between Liz and Rachel, but as a best friend, Liz should stand with me."

"I agree. You've known her much longer than Rachel, although Rachel would be over the moon if you asked her."

"See the dilemma? I don't want to…" I fluttered my hand in the air.

Art groaned. "I see how fast our wedding will take over your life. And you haven't met with Megan yet."

"That's true."

"Megan brought a couple in the other day for rings," Art said. "They're using *Weddings at Wolf Creek Square* as their planner and she mentioned our wedding would be a great marketing feature since we live on the Square."

"I'm afraid she's going to want to showcase everything her business can do for couples and we'll end up with an extravaganza on our hands." I shuddered just thinking about it.

"We have total control, but I agree, we need to know what we want before talking with her. Like I said, whatever you want is fine with me." He squeezed my hand.

I folded the list and slipped it into the pocket of my jacket. His support of my decisions told me everything I needed to know about the man and how lucky I'd been to meet him. That was all well and good, but somehow, I knew our wedding was going to take over my life.

The next morning, Rachel's mind was on Halloween while she fixed breakfast for Thomas. Mornings were always hectic since she made sure he was well fortified before she raced to drop him off at school and began her work at The Inn. "Are you making a new costume this year or a new apron?"

"Carla is going to make matching aprons for us," I said. "She likes the idea of a black top and black pants under the apron."

She slid a scrambled egg onto Thomas' plate, his favorite breakfast. "You seem to like her."

"I do, and training her was easy. She has a similar selling style to mine, so we get along fine."

Rachel grinned. "It's not like having to teach me about quilting, huh?"

I waved her off. "You learned quickly enough. It's hard when everything is new." I swathed my single slice of toast with peanut butter, my standard breakfast fare. "How are your wedding plans coming along?"

"Slow. Both of us are focusing on our jobs right now, along with our new routine with this guy in school." She ruffled Thomas' hair as only mothers can get away with.

"And your plans?"

"Art and I have started. He's going to ask Alan to be his best man. I've decided to ask Liz to stand with me. I hope you understand that I wanted both you and Liz, but Liz has been in my life for a long time. I consider her my best friend. I…I…"

Rachel raised her hand to stop me. "I agree with you. Liz is your best choice. Besides, that will free me to take care of you know who." She smiled and nodded toward Thomas.

"Maybe he'd like to carry the rings?" My suggestion came out of nowhere, but when I said it, I liked the idea.

"See? I'll be busy elsewhere." She stepped forward to give me a hug. "I'll do whatever you need. Get your coat on, Thomas. Time for us to be on our way."

"Yay, I'm going to school." Thomas punched the air and ran from the table to his room.

I felt as if a huge weight had been lifted from my shoulders. Always grateful for her in my life, Rachel made few requests of me. They usually involved taking care of Thomas, but only when I had the time. I was relieved she didn't feel slighted when I told her about Liz.

I was at the front door when Art arrived for our morning walk to B and B for coffee. He greeted me with a kiss and started my day on a happy note. As we neared the coffee shop, I saw Jack and Liz by the front door. I waved, and they waited for us to join them.

"Liz? Before we go inside, can I talk to you?" Art gave me a pat on the shoulder before going inside with Jack.

"Everything okay? Still wearing your ring," she teased, "so I know the wedding's not cancelled."

"Yes, all's fine, but it's about the wedding." I stopped to take a deep breath. "Will you be my matron of honor?"

"Wow." She took in a few gulps of air. "You took my breath away. I thought you'd ask Rachel."

She hadn't answered my question. "Well?" I was getting nervous. Liz was always ready with an answer. "Would you like to be…"

"Gotcha." She laughed. "No other place I'd rather be

than at your side." She leaned in to give me a hug. "Who's Art asking?"

"Alan."

"What about Rachel?" She turned to pull open the door for us to enter.

The strong aroma of coffee greeted us and that sweet, yeasty smell of fresh scones and muffins. Nancy, the morning waitress, waved and held up a mug for each of us. We nodded to let her know we wanted our usual coffee. Liz and I grabbed two of the empty chairs at what had become known as the women's table.

"I told Rachel this morning that I was going to ask you."

"For all the ups and downs you had with her that first year, she has grown into quite a young woman," Liz said.

Before I said more about Rachel, the morning round of wedding questions began. I wanted to get up and leave, but these women were my friends, people I was inviting to my wedding. I answered some in generic terms and others I avoided, especially those about the honeymoon. According to Rachel's brides' magazines, Art was supposed to come up with ideas for that. One of the groom's few official jobs, I'd noted.

When the men got up to leave, I joined Art for the walk back to our end of the Square.

"I heard some of the questions you're dealing with. Sorry our wedding has added to your already busy season," he said.

"Well, lucky for you, I'd marry you even if we didn't live in this community. They're friends and are excited for us, and I've done my share of teasing others when they were getting married."

We bypassed Quilts Galore and Art pulled me over to the front window of Art&Son. His windows looked exactly like he'd described them, but there was one addition. My blue box rested in a bed of straw in the center of one display.

"Oh, I was teasing when I offered it to you." I pointed to the box.

"I know, but with the box in the window you won't be able to put the ring away."

"Smart man." I gave him a kiss and went to unlock my shop door. Carla had arrived and was waiting for me. She carried her Halloween tote, as she did every day.

"Before we get distracted, I'd like to show you my apron design for us," she said.

"And I have a question for you. Would you like to give out the candy this year? One of us needs to be available for shoppers."

The trick-or-treat day was not for shoppers, but I didn't think Carla knew that. It was a time for children to gather candy or small toys in a safe environment. In past years, members of the local police department had dressed in costumes and mingled with the crowd to keep the Square safe for families. Most shopkeepers considered the Halloween event good PR for their businesses.

"Rachel and Thomas will be out and about this year and I can't be in both places."

"Candy? Sure," Carla said. "I'll get to see all those cute little kids in their costumes."

While we were talking, she pulled the two aprons from her tote and handed me one. I couldn't keep my laughter inside. Not one piece was cut square or straight and the pieces were sewn with no sense of design or placement. She'd used many small pieces for the bib and skirt and one large black square for the pocket. She'd added a ruffle to mine, but it only went half-way across the bottom edge. I put it on to model it for her.

"These are wonderful," I said. "So funky and perfect for the day."

"It's kept me busy in the evenings. With it getting dark so early, sometimes the evenings become long."

An idea struck me. "My friend, Liz, has sewn models, small projects, for me, but she's very busy right now and doesn't have any extra time. If we had samples of smaller projects that could be finished by the holidays, I'm sure more fabric would sell."

"I bought a fabric kit a few years ago and was able to put the table runner together quickly when friends asked me to join them for Thanksgiving," Carla said. "It was a great hostess gift."

"See what I mean? You find a couple of patterns you think would sell as kits and choose fabrics to make an eye-catching model to go with the pattern. We have about six weeks before Christmas. You can spread out in the classroom."

"This will be fun." She let her hand rub across the bolts of fabric as she walked past the displays.

I was busy with shoppers all morning, but Carla went back and forth from the shop to the classroom carrying various bolts of fabric, mostly holiday-themed—Thanksgiving as well as Christmas—but also complementary colored small prints and solids. Near noon, I heard the sewing machine whizzing along. My curiosity won out, so when there was a break between customers I wanted to see her choices and went to the classroom.

She'd arranged the fabric bolts in piles as needed for each pattern. Her one sample model was for Thanksgiving with rich colors of rust and amber and merlot red. When I cleared my throat to let her know I was in the room, she turned and grinned sheepishly. "I guess I got carried away. Not often you have a whole quilt shop filled with fabric to use." She allowed a little laugh to escape.

"Not to worry. I would have done the same thing, if I'd had the time. Tell me about your choices." I swept my arm over her groupings.

And she did. Using simple explanations for pattern selection and fabric choices, I could see she had experience with color and fabric combinations. "And this Thanksgiving table runner goes together using straight line sewing, no curves or complicated corners."

She handed me the top for the table runner.

"Wow. Are you this good at planning a wedding?"

"I heard you and Art are getting married, which I think is terrific, but no, I have no experience with weddings. We never had children of our own, but we've enjoyed the weddings of our friends' children."

Our conversation had ventured away from the model and kits so when the bell jingled I told her to cut and package three of each style. I might be selling them in January on the sale table, but then again, other kits had sold in years' past.

Absentmindedly, I carried her model to the front of the shop with me. "Hello, welcome to Quilts Galore. How can I help you?"

The young lady reached out toward the model. "Sell me this." She pulled her hand back. "I'm sorry to be so bold. My in-laws are coming for Thanksgiving and my mother-in-law is one of those women who changes her holiday decorations every month. I'm really nervous about them coming and I need something new."

"Stop. Take a deep breath and let it out. This is a model for the shop, but if you talk to Carla—she's in the classroom— maybe she can make one for you."

The bell on the door jingled frequently that afternoon and I was lost in my world of fabric and quilting. I smiled as each customer left carrying a Quilts Galore shopping bag. Large or small purchase, it didn't matter, they'd come to *my* shop. The frantic woman who wanted to impress her mother-in-law waved and smiled when she left. I guess we'd made her happy.

Carla joined me at the check-out counter and finished filling a bag for me when I handed the shopper her receipt. When the door closed, the smile on Carla's face told me the whole story.

"You didn't have to do that, you know. I told the woman I'd only use Quilts Galore fabric and you would determine the total cost. I have her number next to the sewing machine in the classroom."

"I'll call her after we choose the fabrics."

I remembered making the first quilt as a professional sewer when I lived in Green Bay. I relished the personal pride I felt when my client picked up the quilt and told me she'd tell her friends I made it.

***

Art and I had a bench date that evening. Night arrived before we were finished with the events of our day, but the fairy lights in the courtyard and the light from the antique lamppost lit the area around us. The coolness of the evening finally forced us to say good night.

I went upstairs and found Rachel reading a story to Thomas, who was leaning against her, breathing quietly, his eyes closed. She abruptly stopped reading when I came in.

"He's asleep. I wanted to know how the story ended," Rachel explained with a chuckle.

"So you were reading out loud to yourself?"

"More or less. Okay, I admit it. I miss reading to him at bedtime. Seems like I've done it since he was born, but now I'm not home to put him to bed as often as I want."

I let the comment about her schedule interfering with her time with Thomas hang in the air. It was a problem all single mothers dealt with. Instead, I added, "You also sang to him."

"Haven't done that much lately, either."

"Want help getting him to bed?" I asked.

"Nah, he's not that heavy yet. You off to bed?"

"I suppose. Was there something you needed?"

"A few minutes of your time."

I suspected that was the reason she was still up. "Okay, I'll wait."

Rachel slid Thomas into her arms and padded down the hall to their room. I heard the click of the door before she returned.

I'd grabbed one of the bridal magazines to pass the couple of minutes it took to tuck Thomas in. Rachel came back and folded one leg under her before she sat in the chair opposite the loveseat.

She pointed to the magazine in my lap. "Looking for wedding ideas?"

"All of this is too elaborate for me. I want simple and pretty, not all the glitter and, oh, I don't know, *largeness* they show in their samples." I tossed the magazine onto the coffee table and it pushed one of Thomas' trucks to the edge. Rachel caught it before it toppled over. "What about you and Alan? I assume you're making plans?"

Rachel glanced around the room, looking everywhere

31

but at me. Finally she said, "As much as I'd like a spring wedding, uh, Alan and I aren't sure we can afford one that soon." She stared at the floor and let out a quick, breezy laugh. "Well, at least one that matches all these places our imaginations are taking us."

Rachel's words were so stark and matter-of-fact. She didn't sound like herself at all. Instantly, I began to wonder if it bothered her not having her own mother around during what was supposed to be a happy time. If she'd been living with her mom and stepdad, maybe they'd have paid for at least part of the wedding. Rachel hadn't talked to me, and as far as I knew, Alan hadn't talked to Art about covering some of the cost of the wedding, either. Of course, things had changed. Maybe they assumed they'd pay for the wedding themselves.

Unfortunately, Rachel hadn't seen her mother in years, and only time would tell if Rachel would even invite Lydia to the wedding. I could say with a degree of certainty her mom wouldn't be part of the planning.

"If you're worried about not having the money, remember, you've got your trust fund, although we've always agreed you should be careful about using too much of it."

At the end of his life, William had made sure that his daughter would have money to use for special things, like her education. I had control of that money until Rachel turned twenty-five, when she'd take charge. We'd never spoken about the money after I showed her the documents. She and Thomas lived with me, but she took care of expenses for herself and Thomas out of her salary.

"I'm thinking of that money as for emergencies, Thomas' education, maybe part of a down payment on a house," Rachel said with a shrug, "but not the wedding itself. I guess Alan and I need to make time for these decisions. We're just so busy."

I found it puzzling, even vaguely troubling that they hadn't been planning this all along. I thought they'd simply wanted to keep their ideas to themselves while they worked them out. Now I wasn't so sure. Rachel wasn't all that eager to talk about it.

Art and I still hadn't hashed over living arrangements ourselves, mainly because they weren't likely to be complicated. We'd more or less agreed the kids should have my place and I'd move next door into his apartment. We both wanted to stay on the Square and our shops provided the workspace and storage we needed. On the other hand, Rachel hadn't said anything, so maybe she and Alan had other ideas of their own.

"We'll take these weddings one step at a time, honey, like we've done in the past, but not tonight. A bus tour is coming on Saturday and the shop needs a major primping tomorrow."

Rachel laughed, which had been my purpose in using such an old-fashioned word.

"Right. I've got an early meeting with Gwen and Ashley. Events and room reservations need to be streamlined and Cameron decided to keep the banquet room available if it rains during the Halloween festival."

"That's thoughtful of him."

Rachel shook her head. "True enough, but it's on a Saturday, our busiest day. We already have four events scheduled."

"Between the three of you, I'm sure they will all go smoothly and no one will notice that you changed the rooms." I don't know why I said that. How would I know how they'd juggle their events?

Rachel stood and bent forward to give me a hug. "Love you, 'night."

"Same from me to you." I straightened the magazines and folded the couch quilt I'd pulled over me while we talked. I turned off the lights and looked out the window to the small town that had become my home. I thought about my years in this apartment over my shop and Art right next door. Hmm…that would change, of course, but I'd love wherever we lived as long as we were together.

3

I was in the middle of rearranging bolts of fabric when Carla arrived and said her happy hello, her way to start the day at Quilts Galore in an upbeat mood. Then she moved between displays of fabric to the classroom where she put her lunch in the fridge.

"What's the order for today?" she asked, which told me she was ready to begin.

I handed her a list of five jobs. "These need to be done soon, preferably before Saturday's bus tour. Remember the Boy Scout motto?"

"Absolutely," she said, scanning the paper. "Be prepared."

"But first, and it's not on the list, we need more kits put together," I said. "We have only two left from the first batch you made. Use your creativity. Don't bother asking me if I like your fabric choices. They'll sell, either now or in January."

The bell jingled, starting the day on a good note. Carla wandered over to help the customer.

My job that morning involved unpacking and entering into the computer the shipment that had arrived the previous afternoon. For years, Rachel had handled all the new shipments because she had better computer skills. I had learned to fend for myself when she got her job with Hutch Hotels.

I'd always found the unpacking to be like Christmas morning, with every box containing gifts. Sure, the thread and notions were standard items that never changed, but the fabric? Pure fun. Some of the bolts I'd ordered were basic colors and patterns, but, being on the program of automatic shipments meant some surprises.

In the middle of the third box of fabric I pulled out a bolt that made me pause. I unfolded the beginning yardage so I could see more of the design. Stamped on the dark blue—almost midnight blue background—were silver sleigh bells, singly and in groups of two or three. Each bell sported a ribbon bow in the same silver color.

I immediately liked the idea of silver bells as a wedding theme. My ideas came quickly, so I grabbed my notebook and scribbled them down; dress colors, table decorations, ring pillow, candles, invitations. I couldn't stop.

Carla stood in the door way. "Marianna, could you help me?" Her arms were filled with bolts of fabric.

"Sure." I stashed my notebook in my pocket. Even if I lost it, I wouldn't forget my ideas. They'd come with such clarity I was never going to forget them. I was surprised to find the shop had quilters in every corner. I had been so distracted with the fabric I'd not heard the bell jingle. No wonder Carla was a little breathless.

I headed in the direction of the voice calling, "Can someone help me?"

Working in tandem, Carla and I saw that every woman left with a Quilts Galore bag in her hand. I did a high-five with Carla and told her that she was an asset to the shop. "You could have called me sooner, you know." I spoke with a wry smile, so she wouldn't take the words as criticism.

"Haven't gotten to the kits yet, but I'll start right now." She didn't respond to my comment.

"I'd like your opinion first." I motioned for Carla to follow me and walked toward the classroom.

I ran my hand over the fabric I'd found. "This fabric was in the shipment and I think it would work as a theme for my wedding." I unfolded a few yards of the bolt. I wanted her honest opinion, not just to agree with me because I couldn't stop smiling. I described my ideas and she nodded in agreement with each one. "I'll be asking Liz and Rachel their opinion, too, so don't be shy about your answer."

"I was wondering what you'd do. Time's getting short to put an elaborate wedding together."

"That's not my style. I want it simple and nice. Most of all, I want the guests to have a good time, like they're at a fun party."

"I'm all for that. For a second marriage, I think your idea is perfect. But I'm wasting time and kits have to be made."

I laughed and waved her away. I touched the blue fabric, smoothed the edges as I rewound it on the bolt. I took a few minutes to take the bolt and put it in my room upstairs for safe keeping. Before going back down, I sent a text to Art. Color theme chosen. I added a heart.

My daydreaming was over when the bell jingled on my way downstairs. I became Marianna Spencer, shopkeeper instead of Marianna Spencer, bride-to-be. But the thought of being a bride stayed with me as the afternoon passed by.

Carla was preparing to leave for the day when I noticed six more kits were on display by the model she'd made. "Thanks for finishing the kits. I'm sure they'll sell."

"Let's hope so. Lots of cut fabric to use if they don't." She reached in her tote for her keys. "Um…what do you think about wearing our Halloween aprons on Saturday? The customers will see we're part of the shop."

"Great idea. Too much work to only use them one day. Let's start wearing them tomorrow."

A huge smile crossed her face. "See you then." The bell jingled when she pulled the door closed.

I turned the bolt to lock the door and was about to climb the steps when someone knocked on the front door. I noticed her arms were loaded with bags from other shops on the Square. I released the lock and opened the door.

"I'm sorry it's after hours, but I got waylaid at each shop I visited. I only heard about Wolf Creek Square yesterday," the woman said. "I'm visiting family and we're leaving in the morning and won't be back 'til next year. Would you let me spend a few minutes looking?"

Selling was the name of the game and she seemed ready

to buy. "Please look around." I waved her in, and she parked her bags inside the door.

I kept busy, adding the new bolts of fabric to the displays. Every now and then, I heard an "oh" or an "ah." I smiled to myself at the sounds. She might have been tasting delectable chocolate cake or a melt-in-your-mouth cookie. *Food or fabric, whatever touches your soul.* I quickly jotted the saying in my notebook. Maybe I'd use it in a promotion or partner with Steph at B and B or with Melanie at Crossroads for a coupon.

The shopper piled six bolts of fabric on the cutting table and two of Carla's newly cut kits. "I'll take half a yard of each of these and the kits." She stopped to take a breath. "I'll be back with more." She spun around and went to a different part of the shop. She immediately came back. "Are the fabrics in the classroom for sale?"

I thought of my bolt of Silver Bells resting safely on my bed upstairs. "Yup. I just unpacked them today, so you're the first to see them."

She looked at her phone. "I just called my family and they'll hold dinner an hour for me, so cut fast."

Shoppers under pressure bought on impulse and didn't spend time debating color or design. In the end, her pressure was going to be my reward. I began to cut with focus.

She brought bolts from every display and didn't hesitate to consider her choices. She wanted fabric. Three more kits hit the pile. Her face was red with excitement. "Do you mail order if I send a swatch?"

"Some of the bolts are a one-time order, but if I have it in stock, sure." I could talk while I cut. I'd honed that skill after buying the shop and working alone much of the time.

I heard the bell jingle. I waved Art over and asked him to load the shopping bags with her fabric. The kits fit in two more bags. In the end, the woman left with four bags on her arm from Quilts Galore, in addition to the bags she'd come in with. Art locked the door when she left.

"I'd hate to see her credit card total for the day." Art leaned in for a kiss. "She bought six of my brooches and two of Alan's necklaces."

"Wow. Don't you love these days when something unplanned happens?"

"I love each day I can be with you, Marianna," Art said. "Dinner? I've got news."

"Me, too. Let's go before Crossroads fills up." I pulled my apron off and tossed it on the cutting table.

I locked the door behind us. A swatch of the Silver Bells fabric I cut off earlier was in my pocket, but I wanted to hear Art's news first.

Our favorite table had a family of four sitting at it, so Art chose a table in the corner away from most of the guests. We each ordered the special of the day—Cauldron Stew, Scarecrow Green Salad, and a pumpkin-shaped cookie frosted in orange.

"Tell me your news first," I said. "I need to hear your voice tonight." His rich, tenor voice had attracted me to him from the beginning.

He reached across the table for my hand. "You won't like it."

"The sun doesn't shine every day," I said, "to quote Sadie."

He drew in a breath. "I don't know how this happened. I thought I was keeping ahead of the game, but after that woman in your shop bought six brooches, I found I didn't have enough in reserve to fill the empty spaces in the display cases."

"So make some more," I said lightly. "You always do."

"Easy for you to say. We've talked about spending more evenings together than we usually do, what with wedding plans and such. Now I'm behind and the holidays loom." He sat back in his chair when the waitress served our food. "I need to spend more evenings making enough pieces to get me through the holidays."

"*Every* evening?" I winced at the whine in my voice.

His laughter made me smile. "No, no, I'm not that dedicated. I just mean I have to put in more hours. I try to stay out of Alan's way when he's working on his jewelry. He still carries a little fear that I'll judge his work."

"But you don't, do you?"

"Nope. Based on the number of necklaces he sells, I have no right to comment at all. He's developed a following of clients that will only work with him now. They don't even want to talk to me." He pulled the corners of his mouth down to make a *poor me* face.

I patted his hand. "I know, poor you. But speaking of Alan, has he mentioned anything about their wedding?"

Art finished his bite of stew before answering. "Nothing specific, at least not lately. He's been asking more about our plans? What about Rachel?"

I frowned. "She told me she'd like a spring wedding, but then said money is a problem. That seemed very odd. She said they don't know where they'll live, but obviously we can solve that problem quickly enough. Or, maybe they want to get a place around the Square." I shrugged. "Just seems strange they say so little about when they'll get married. I wonder if Rachel's feeling bad about being estranged from her mom."

"Could be," Art said. He quickly added, "But maybe they don't want to talk about their plans since our wedding is coming up fast. You know, they don't want to overshadow us. Maybe that's it."

"Well, like you said, could be. Then we should reassure them that we're as interested in their plans as our own."

"We are?" Art laughed as if he'd made a joke. Then he softened his tone. "I suppose. But, how about we leave them to figure things out. They know we're here to help."

Something about Art's teasing tone rubbed me the wrong way. "It seems you're telling me to mind my own business."

"Oh, not really, Marianna. It's just that worrying about them doesn't help anything. Besides, seems to me they're acting pretty responsible."

Like Rachel, Art didn't sound like himself. Usually, I was the one who had to urge him to back off and let Alan make his own decisions. Now the tables had turned.

Art held up the pumpkin cookie. "Wanna bet Steph made these?" He winked.

I laughed. "Why would I bet knowing I'd lose?"

"Spoil sport." Art grinned, then shifted in his chair. "I'm

really sorry about limiting the amount of time we can spend together. I don't like the idea of losing any of dessert and coffee dates…but…"

"Oh, please. I'm a shopkeeper. I know every day can't be 10:00 to 6:00. We don't lock the door and call it a day, especially from now until the end of the year." I flashed a sly grin. "At which point, we'll be married, anyway."

Art tapped his temple. "That's why I love you." He refilled our cups while the waitress cleared our plates. "Now, your turn. What's this about a color theme for the wedding?"

"With our wedding following on the heels of Christmas, I wanted something unusual but still festive." I reached into my pocket to show him the fabric sample. "See? Not red or green like Christmas and nothing like New Year's. To me, these are wedding bells, only in silver instead of white. You see? Silver Bells."

Art nodded. "It suits you, Marianna."

I was on a roll and all my ideas tumbled out as I described the banquet room with round tables, dark blue and silver flowers in silver vases and on and on until Art quietly said, "Enough…you've made the sale."

I took one last breath and said, "Invitations?"

Art frowned, as if thinking hard. "Uh, let me take care of that."

I trusted him as an artist to design a unique way to invite our friends to share our day. I wouldn't pester him, knowing the pressure he was under to make brooches and rings for the holidays. I hoped he wouldn't forget, because my worry barometer had already kicked into high gear.

***

The day of the Fall Color bus tour Carla came in early. "I didn't sleep much last night, wondering if I'd be up for the high intensity shoppers today." She looked out the window. "I don't think they'll see much color here though. Most of the leaves have fallen from the trees."

I was surprised at her concern. Carla had been ready to tackle any job I gave her. "I'm sure you'll do fine, but if you need a break, go into the classroom and close the door for a few minutes."

That was the last time Carla and I said more than a few quick phrases to each other until the final group of women from the bus tour left Quilts Galore.

"Well, did you survive?" I teased, taking advantage of the break to lean on the counter.

"What a rush of people," Carla said, wide-eyed. "I'm sure glad I know something about quilting so I could answer their questions. These women are power shoppers."

"Many have been here before, so they know what I carry."

"I was surprised how many asked about Liz and Rachel," she remarked.

"They worked for me early on, and then later, mostly during busy times. They have other jobs now." I told her about the lady from the evening before. "You should have seen her walk away *loaded down* with shopping bags from most of the shops, but especially mine."

"Oh, I wish I had been here to see it," Carla said, "but I knew something grand had happened when I checked on the kits and all but two were gone."

"Would you like to do another sample for the shop with a Thanksgiving theme and maybe a simple tree skirt or stocking for Christmas? We want to move more of those fabrics before the end of the year."

"More sewing, more fun. I plan to get that lady's table runner done over the weekend."

I turned away when my phone rang, glad to see Beverly returned my call. After we exchanged greetings, I said, "I'm sure you heard that Art and I are getting married the Saturday following Christmas. I need a dress, but am I too late for you and Virgie to create an original for me?"

"White with lots of lace and beadwork?" She chuckled.

"Silly lady. Simple lines, soft fabric, blue and silver. I have a sample of the fabric I'm going to use as an accent."

"Would it be all right if I stopped by in about fifteen minutes? I'm around the corner at Styles and am heading home," Beverly said. "I can talk with Virgie tonight and give you an answer tomorrow."

"I'll be here. Thanks." As an afterthought, I dialed Liz to see if she could join us. I wanted her dress to complement mine but not overshadow the design. Since she'd been at Country Law waiting for Jack to finish with a client, she was happy to come right over.

Beverly and Liz walked in together as Carla left with a wave.

"Virgie and I are sewing beads on a wedding dress tonight, so I can't stay long," Beverley said. "Show me your fabric and tell me your ideas."

I unfolded the swatch of fabric and described a two-layered dress—blue over silver with the overskirt swaged up to the waist at the side letting the silver underskirt show. A blue bodice for the dress with a small silver jacket tailored enough for my conservative style, but still with a party flair.

Beverly nodded. "That's easy for us to do and the blue and silver are standard colors, so the fabric won't need to be a special order." She turned to Liz. "And for you?"

Liz was known for her bright colors and trendy styles, but I was hoping she'd consider a more reserved style for my wedding.

"I haven't given it much thought." She gave me a quizzical look. "Have you?"

"Not until I saw this fabric," I said. "I'm no designer, but how about a simple shift in blue and a flowing silver jacket with alternating panels of blue and silver for the back, and well…maybe a blue cuff on the sleeves."

Bev made notes as I spoke, and even managed a few sketches. I had no idea where my ideas came from, but once I started to describe them, I liked them both. Liz seemed to as well.

"These are easy for us to do. Like I said, I'll talk to Virgie tonight and then we'll need measurements before we order the fabric." She put her notebook into her purse. "We have wedding dresses and attendants' outfits, as well as consignment pieces for New Year's that are in line ahead of your dresses. But don't worry. Once those orders are done, we'll get to yours."

Bev left first, on her way to Country Law where her sewing

partner and housemate worked as the receptionist. Virgie did most of the designing and Bev sewed the garments. They had quite the business with Styles exclusively offering their wedding dresses and vests.

Liz gave me a quick shoulder hug. "That was easier than I anticipated. I thought we'd be going through wedding and fashion magazines for weeks." She slung the straps of her purse on her shoulder. "When did all these ideas hit you?"

"I saw the fabric and wham, the ideas kept flowing. I guess looking at all those bridal magazines upstairs triggered my creativity. Now I need to talk to Megan. You up for that conversation so we can keep her reined in?"

"I'll make time," Liz said with a grin. "My best friend doesn't get married every day. Give Megan a call, then let me know the details."

On that note she gave me a hug and hurried off to Country Law to collect her husband. Rachel and Thomas, running at full speed and waving a drawing, came in after she left.

"Look, look, Nana. We made pumpkin pictures today," Thomas said. "Can we put it on the fridge?"

He handed me his art work. "You bet. We need new pictures to brighten our home."

He ran upstairs ahead of us.

It was a rare occurrence for the three of us to be home for supper at the same time. Rachel had to be at The Inn some evenings. Then, either Alan took care of Thomas and made sure he had dinner, or I did, which gave me extra time with him.

We fixed one of our favorite quick suppers of pancakes and scrambled eggs. After Thomas tried to tell us about his pumpkin drawing for the third time, Rachel pointed to their room.

"Time for a bath and brushing teeth, buddy. Call me and we'll read a story." She held up her index finger. "One story."

Thomas touched my arm, probably hoping I'd take his side and let him stay up later, but I never interfered with Rachel's rules for Thomas. I only gave my opinion on anything involved with raising him when Rachel specifically asked.

"Better hurry, Thomas, or there won't be time for a story." I gave him a hug and said good night.

Having exhausted his options, he gave a quick, "Night, Nana," and off he ran. Bedtime stories were an important part of his day. Many mornings, he'd tell me all about the story from the night before.

I went to my room and changed clothes and later, Rachel and I met up in the kitchen to clean up the dinner dishes.

"Boy, I wish I had that energy at the end of the day," Rachel said as she rinsed our dinner plates and put them in the dishwasher while I put away the jam and syrup, and took a quick inventory of our supplies. We were low on milk. I added it to our growing grocery list we'd hung on the refrigerator door, a pen on a string taped next to it.

Looking at the calendar, I said, "I see you're working late on Monday, so why don't I pick up Thomas at Sally's and take him grocery shopping with me." Thomas had gone to Sally's Day Care since he was a tiny baby, and now he enjoyed her after-school program.

Rachel finished loading the dishwasher and added three more items to the list. "No, it's my turn. I'll arrange to do it over the weekend. I'll be at The Inn after hours on Monday with Megan to go over a Halloween wedding table layout. Alan has a late meeting with Cameron."

I scrunched my nose. "Who would want to be married on Halloween?"

"Some spooky couple." Rachel chuckled. "Megan said the guests are coming in costumes. Should be interesting."

I couldn't hold back a snicker. "Can't imagine looking at those pictures twenty-five years from now. And having that wedding photo on your mantle, basically forever."

"Me, either. Different people, different tastes, I guess." Rachel folded the towel and hung it on the rack. She liked a clean kitchen and ours shined. "Have you called Megan yet?"

"No, I've been avoiding her until I had ideas. I'll call her on Monday. Art wants to focus on his inventory and told me to go ahead with whatever needs to be done."

"Who's performing the ceremony?"

Rachel heard Thomas call before I answered. She waved when she left the room.

"Thanks for reminding me," I said, grabbing my phone. I tapped Jack's number.

"I've a question for you," I said after he answered. "Maybe Art should be asking you this, but…can you officiate at our wedding?"

Silence.

"Jack?"

"Um…you see…oh, no. I wish this hadn't happened, but I'll be busy that day. Out of town. But it's no problem. Richard is authorized to perform weddings in Wisconsin."

"You're busy? But Jack, it's my wedding day."

"I'd like to explain, but I can't, Marianna. You know, attorney-client stuff. I wish…"

This made no sense at all. I could feel myself reacting with a strange mix of anger and disappointment. "Well, okay then. I'll guess I'll call Richard." I ended the call abruptly and turned off the kitchen light.

It was still early, but I was tired and didn't feel like starting a movie. Jack's news seemed to drain the energy right out of me. As I readied for bed, I thought about calling Art and telling him I wouldn't be at morning coffee. I'd left shop cleanup for the morning, but I didn't want to interrupt his work time. I sent a quick text. I really wanted to tell him about Jack's odd response when I'd asked him to officiate. He and Liz were my oldest friends. It made no sense. It hurt.

As I climbed into bed, I thought about the changes coming. Art and I had different rhythms to our businesses. His jewelry made perfect last-minute gifts. He sold brooches and rings right up until he closed on Christmas Eve. My shop was busier in the fall leading up to the holidays. Not that I didn't sell plenty of gift certificates and the few finished quilts I stocked, but most of my shoppers were quilters themselves and they needed their supplies in the summer and fall.

Art and I had adjusted for all these years, so I was sure

we'd find our way easily enough when we lived together. Compromises were part of two people living together.

I drifted off to sleep with Art on my mind and was awakened in the morning by his voice on the phone calling to tell me he wouldn't be at coffee, either. His kiln had malfunctioned and ruined a batch of brooches. He had a long day ahead remaking them. Nothing for either of us to do but get ready for another busy day.

4

The morning of the Halloween Party started as spooky as a traditional horror story. A strong wind blew the last of the leaves around the courtyard, forcing me to overlap the fronts of my heavy sweater as Art and I headed hand in hand to B and B for coffee, talking about the threat of rain.

"I'm declaring no rain and maybe a little sunshine by afternoon," I said in an authoritative voice. "No one is going to rain on Thomas' parade, not even Mother Nature."

"Right. You put in your weather order and we'll see what's delivered." Art always laughed at my tendency to demand the weather I wanted. "Alan asked me to wave when I saw Thomas pass by in the parade. I get a kick out of Alan talking about Thomas' first bike and setting up a college fund for him."

"Seems he's always been like a dad to Thomas," I said, "even back when he and Rachel were just kids themselves."

We were within a few steps of entering the coffee shop when Art said, "Alan wanted my thoughts about him making it legal with Thomas. You know, actually adopting him after he and Rachel are married."

"I'm not surprised. I imagine you weren't, either. He's always been in Thomas' life, practically since the day we moved here."

Art nodded. "Funny, though, I still think of Alan as much younger than he actually is. The years have passed so quickly."

"From what people say, that's a normal reaction of parents. You put in all that work—alone, for much of the time—and managed to keep him safe and happy. No wonder the time flew by."

When we went inside, I noticed Steph had a witch's hat on and Nancy had dyed her hair pink. I'd left my apron at the shop, so dressed in my black turtleneck and black pants, I looked like a half-dressed ninja. My black sweater added to my shadowy appearance.

The weather was the topic-of-the-day at the women's table, but we veered from there to the latest shipment of holiday clothes, especially the sparkly dresses Styles was featuring in their window.

"You all have to see the newest vest designs by Bev and Virgie. They are so stylish I may have to buy one myself." Mimi was more animated than usual that morning. She'd always been the quietist among the boisterous shopkeepers that gathered at Biscuits and Brew.

Skylar, from The Toy Box, was having a private discussion with her grandmother, Millie, the owner of BookMarks. Claire, Millie's sister, was a morning coffee regular, too. She'd lived a nomadic life before coming to Wolf Creek Square to be with her sister. I considered us fortunate to have her among us. The two of us had become good friends.

Even chatty Megan seemed to be preoccupied on her phone. I hadn't seen her so serious in a long time, but the frustration on her face left no question that the call was important. She was texting a reply as fast as her fingers could spell the words.

Georgia Reynolds made a rare appearance that morning. Her home life kept her busy. She was married to Elliot Reynolds from Farmer Foods, but they also raised horses and had a bunch of mares and foals at their house at the farm. She worked as a paralegal at Country Law so free time was a premium.

Georgia pulled a chair next to me and held up two fingers. "Two quick questions. First, why haven't you told us about Carla? She stopped to buy groceries and told Elliot she was happy working at Quilts Galore."

I shrugged, puzzled by such a trivial question. "I don't know—"

Georgia interrupted, apparently not that interested in an answer. "And wedding plans, Marianna. You haven't shared any of your details with us. Are you keeping it all top secret in case you decide not to marry Art?"

Laughing, I almost choked on a sip of coffee. "No, nothing that drastic. I'm like everyone else around here, getting ready for the holidays. Until the other day, I didn't have any plans to discuss."

The others around the table were looking on, as if waiting for more. "Hey, everyone's busy around here," I said, pointing to Liz. "Look at how busy Liz is with Sarah's books…"

"I sure am," Liz agreed in a firm tone.

"And between The Inn and Thomas," I said, "Rachel's schedule is full. I needed help and one day Carla came in and asked for a job. She's been quilting for years and seems to enjoy working with the customers. As for the wedding, Art and I want something much simpler than what Rachel's brides' magazines show."

Megan was off her phone and now listening to the conversation.

"But until I speak with my wedding planner, I'm not giving out any details." I cupped my ear. "Do you hear me, Megan? I'll be calling for an appointment with you."

Megan grinned. "I'm here for you."

When we noticed the men had started gathering their plates and cups, it was a signal for us women to head out ourselves and get our shops open for business.

"I can reveal a little about the wedding," I said.

"Really?" Georgia asked.

"That's right. You're all invited. Art's in charge of invitations so don't be afraid to bug him about details." I stacked my mug on my plate and headed to the dirty dish bin by the door.

Bits of sunshine greeted us outside, giving us hope that our biggest children's event on the Square all year wouldn't be moved inside due to weather.

Megan nudged me from behind. "I'll be waiting for your call, Marianna. I'm sure we can find a time to meet."

We both knew it wouldn't be easy. We had full days and evenings as the shops on the Square started to move deeper into holiday mode. But, with both of us studying our calendars, we finally found a night the next week when she could stop by my place late in the evening. Megan warned me that we didn't have much time to plan, especially if I wanted what she called little details for our guests.

With a light laugh I said, "Think simple, Megan. We have plenty of time." Who was the wedding planner here? I knew the kind of wedding I wanted and if it was going to take me extra time to keep Megan on track than that was what I'd do.

***

By mid-afternoon, the sun was bright overhead and the Square was filled with families ready to trick-or-treat. A children's costume parade would come before the candy giving began. The planners also arranged for a man dressed in patched clothes to walk through the courtyard, blowing up long skinny balloons and then twisting them into animal shapes. He was giving them to the children.

When Thomas, looking cute in his clown costume, passed Quilts Galore he ran up the steps and handed me his balloon dog. "Keep it safe, Nana."

Then he ran back to join his friends in the parade. The second time around the courtyard, the children gathered around Carla to get their candy. She didn't have children or grandchildren, but she knew how to rave about the costumes and make each child feel special. With no shoppers around, I was free to stand by the door and listen to her laugh as she added an extra piece of candy to their bags.

With dusk approaching, the parents and kids began drifting away. It wasn't long before the Square was quiet and dark again.

Quiet wasn't the operative word when Alan and Rachel brought Thomas home. "Nana, look in my bag. See? It's not all candy that Mom will take away. Clayton gave us a coloring book and pencils, and Millie gave each of us a book."

He pulled the book from his bag and handed it to Rachel. "The story for tonight, Mom."

"Okay," she said, "but it's late. Better go get ready for bed."

"Candy, Mom?"

I could see Thomas knew he was pushing his luck, but was bold enough on Halloween to take a chance.

Rachel planted her hands on her hips. "Oh, all right. Three *small* pieces."

He reached into the bag Alan was holding and ran up the stairs to his room.

"I wonder how much sugar he's had today," Rachel mused. "You should take some home, Carla. He doesn't need all this."

Carla laughed. "Oh, no you don't. I don't want any candy in my house. Save it for Thomas. That's part of Halloween. Don't you remember?"

As far as I knew, neither Alan nor Rachel had particularly good childhood memories of Halloween. At least I'd never heard them banter about Halloweens of years ago. But when I took pictures of them, I knew they'd have this year's celebration to remember.

Alan offered Carla a weak smile. "I remember the year I used a sheet and cut holes in it to be a ghost. Oops, should have asked Dad. He was a little mad I took the good sheet off my bed and not some old one."

Carla laughed, and so did I. Alan, always a good communicator, covered what could have been an awkward moment.

"So, I'll be on my way," Carla said, "and thanks for letting me be part of this party."

The sound of "Mom" coming from upstairs brought an end to our Halloween.

"I'll walk you to your car," Alan said. "No telling what may be lurking in the corners." He raised his arms and growled like a gorilla, and then gave Rachel a quick kiss, the last of the day for them.

I locked the door.

Rachel rolled her eyes and headed upstairs when Thomas

called a second time.

I was about to turn off the lights when Art knocked on the door. I opened it and stood back to welcome him. "Tell me all about your day."

"Fun as always," he said. "Kids just want to be silly and goofy. Halloween is always a good time to set kids' imaginations free. Something we adults need to do more often. Like a quick dance around the bolts."

I laughed when he grabbed my arm and we danced around a display of autumn and Thanksgiving fabrics, and then made a quick left toward the Christmas fabric. He stopped and sent me spinning under his arm.

He took a step away and bowed. "Seen Alan lately?"

"He's walking Carla to her car."

Art took another bow. "I trained him well."

We both startled when Alan knocked on the front door and Carla was with him. Art opened the door to let them in.

"Carla has a flat tie so I'm going to give her a ride home and she'll have the garage fix it tomorrow. Just wanted you to know, Dad."

Carla said she might be a few minutes late in the morning, but I knew we could work around it. She said good night again and followed Alan back outside.

"That's my cue to leave, too." Art reached out and turned the lights off and drew me close. His sugar high had turned to passion and I was on the receiving end. Lucky me, I got the treat, not the trick.

November
5

As we always did on the first day of the month, Rachel and I coordinated our calendars, a trickier challenge now that she worked for The Inn and Thomas was in school. Rachel, Alan, Art, and I formed the primary members of the village that raised this particular child. Lucky for all of us, Thomas was a stunning example of an easy child to care for, unless he was sick or out-of-sorts. That was my term for times he needed a day with Mom or if he was lucky that day, his mom and Alan.

Rachel and I sat at the kitchen table with our open laptops and studied our schedules, and groaned. Neither one of us had a free day. In addition to the daily appointments and work, the Harvest Festival was the week before Thanksgiving, which was stacked with Black Friday and Small Business Saturday.

"No rest for us Spencer women." Rachel sighed.

I grinned. Rachel was always quick to be positive about our busy lives. Her life was full, and like mine, happy. "Like I always tell Art, I wouldn't have it any other way."

"Don't forget your wedding plans," Rachel said. "Is Megan onboard yet?"

"I plan to call her today, but frankly, I'm not sure she'll do what I ask. When I talked with her briefly, she didn't seem to be listening to my desire for simple and elegant. She seems so intent on our wedding being a showcase for the Wolf Creek wedding business."

"Just keep telling her exactly what you want," Rachel said. "She may suggest something you haven't thought of, either. Just think what wedding planners keep track of."

"Her job can't be easy, that's for sure."

Rachel suddenly closed her program on her tablet and gave me a hug. "Oops, look at the time." She called to Thomas, who was running a truck across the living room rug. "Better put that away now. Time for us to go, buddy."

"Bye, Nana." He raced to the stairs, then turned around and ran back to his room. When he returned, I saw he had his backpack over one shoulder.

"Have a good day, both of you." The apartment went from high volume noise to silence. Not looking forward to making my call to Megan, I had procrastinated long enough. I picked up my phone and placed the call.

Megan croaked out a "hello."

"Megan? What's the matter?"

"Must be a cold coming on. Sore throat, and I'm so achy."

"We can schedule an appointment another time." I wasn't happy my friend was sick, but I was just as happy to avoid an appointment that day.

"I sure can't do it today." A muffled cough came through the phone.

"No, no, we'll do it soon, though. Whenever you're ready." Now wasn't that a twist? I'd been putting her off but now decided it was important for us to meet. Maybe I needed to go back and read that article on wedding anxiety I'd skipped over.

I called Art and whined the best I could about not meeting Megan.

He listened patiently and said, "Don't worry. We've got plenty of time. I'm sure...oops, there goes the buzzer on the kiln. Need to go, love ya'."

"Some morning this is turning out to be," I grumbled to myself as I went downstairs. Maybe Carla would brighten my day.

No such luck.

She complained about the cost of having the tire on her

car fixed and the towing charges. "Back in the old days, garages came out and got your car. It was part of the service, a sign of good will."

I tried to sound neutral when I said, "Nothing stays the same, and that's true in Quilts Galore, too. I'm going to work on the new window display. I want you to move the Halloween fabric away from the front door and replace it with the Christmas fabric."

"That won't take very long to do. Anything else?" Carla said flatly, apparently not interested in that job.

"Books and patterns always need straightening, and the notions rack needs refilling."

Carla looked toward the front door as if wishing a customer would enter. "Maybe we'll make a big sale today."

I gathered my box for the display and headed to the window, leaving Carla to choose which job she wanted to do first.

Pat came in trying to catch her breath, like she'd run across the courtyard. "Change of plans today, Marianna. Two unscheduled buses have arrived. It was easier for me to let everyone know in person than hope you'd check your phone. Have a good day." Out the door she went.

Carla smiled broadly. I suppose she thought her wish for a sale had been prophetic. Maybe it would turn out that way, maybe not. We'd have to wait and see.

"Let's get into action, Carla," I said, my mood lifting. Nothing like a couple of buses loaded with shoppers to keep me focused. "We need more shopping bags from the storage cabinets in the classroom and let's clear off the cutting table." I stepped over to the check-out area and added business cards to the small fabric basket by the register. After Carla stashed the bags under the counter, I handed her an apron.

"We need to wear aprons today—our November aprons." I handed her one. "Liz used to wear this one."

Laughing, Carla quickly put it on. "Thanks. I'm honored."

And so it began. The bell on the door jingled many times during the morning and into late afternoon. The few times I noticed Carla I could see she was in her element and having a lot of fun.

I was enjoying myself, too, at least until a shopper approached, looking grim. "That lady," she said, turning to point to Carla, "said I could have this fabric." She hugged the bolt to her chest.

"I saw it before you did." That came from the woman standing behind the first shopper.

I took the bolt and saw it was almost full. Probably enough to go around. "How many yards do you want?" I asked the first lady.

"Two, maybe three."

"And you?" I inquired of the second.

"I'll take one yard," she said, "but I don't want to buy the same fabric she does because we share cuts of fabric, and we can't share the same fabric."

I stifled a laugh. Customers could be the strangest people. To resolve the "crisis" I found a bolt of the same design in a different color. "Will this solve the problem?"

"Sure. It will for me." The first lady took the bolt of pink fabric—the second choice.

"Me, too." The other lady carried the original bolt of green fabric under her arm.

With that problem resolved, I returned to the cutting table to find a line of women waiting. "Sorry about the delay. Who's next?"

Six bolts hit the table. "One yard of each, please. This is a wonderful shop. I've taken one of your business cards and signed up for your newsletter."

"Did I hear newsletter?" a customer called out. "Where do I sign up?"

Other questions rippled down the line.

Early in my shopkeeping days, I learned the skill of multitasking. Since the woman wanted one yard of each, I layered the six fabrics on top of each other and made one cut. I'd saved a lot of time doing that over the years.

I directed all the shoppers to the newsletter sign-up book by the register and continued to cut fabric and answer questions until the line ended.

In the midst of the flurry, Alan came in to lend a hand, asking for the code to enter the check-out register. Alan was a great end man for a sale. He had a natural talent for customer service and had the ability to make each shopper feel special. He never missed encouraging them to "come back again."

"You need to change the receipt paper soon, Marianna," he said when the crowd had thinned. "I have to get back to work next door, though."

Then, as fast as he came in, he left. As a future son-in-law or maybe stepson-in-law was the correct term, since he was marrying my stepdaughter, I couldn't do better.

At closing time, after the last customer left Quilts Galore, I found Carla replacing the bolts of fabric into their proper displays.

I casually asked, "Did you get the notions' spinner filled?" Then I laughed. As if she'd had the time to do that.

"Now I can really fill it," she said with a quick chuckle. "I had to go into the storeroom and get quilting needles for two of the ladies."

"We have two more tour buses due on Saturday, so we know what we'll be busy with tomorrow." I stretched my arms over my head to give myself a shot of energy. "It's been a great day, so go home and put your feet up."

"I'm sorry about complaining this morning about my flat tire." Carla frowned. "Helping these women reminded me why I asked for the job in the first place. I just wish I could see some of the projects when they finish them."

"That's the downside for this kind of shop. Maybe I need to put up a photo board, so customers can send us a picture of the items they made from supplies they bought here."

She handed me Liz's apron. "Tell her it brought us luck today."

I locked the door, turned off the lights and called Art. I wanted to share my day with him. One ring, two rings, three rings, then a hurried, "Hi."

"Time for C and D tonight around 7:00?" I asked.

"Will be wonderful to see you."

"I'll be on the bench."

***

After the short walk to Crossroads, we settled into chairs at "our" table. Art wasted no time reaching into the inner pocket of his sport coat and pulling out a handful of sketches he'd done for a new signature line of brooches. A few years ago, he'd done a series he called Crowns. Now he'd had numerous requests for another series.

Art spread them out in front of me. "Now, when I draw the next series I'll be sitting across the table from you. Just think, you'll be able to give me instant feedback and tell me if you like them—or not."

I drew back. "Whoa…I'll do no such thing. That would be like asking you to critique one of my original quilt designs. No way will that be part of our marriage."

"Uh oh," Art said, chuckling. "Maybe we need to answer more of those questions from the other night. You know, those from the bridal magazine."

"Getting cold feet, Mr. Carlson? Did I ask the wrong man to marry me?" I teased.

Art put up his hands in surrender. "No more of that kind of talk. I was just suggesting we could learn more about each other's specialty. Not that we don't already know a lot."

"Oh, I'm interested in doing that. But I do want to tell you about Alan coming into the shop and helping me out today."

I sat back and waited to continue while the waitress put down plates of pumpkin chiffon pie and coffee. The dollop of whipped cream on the pie was dusted with nutmeg. Art was quick to skim a thin layer of the cream from my pie while the waitress filled our cups. I pretended to be mad, and so our game went.

"Do tell," he said. "Alan and I are like ships passing in the night lately."

This wasn't the first time Art heard about Alan showing up at the perfect time, lending a hand, and then going on his way. I didn't leave out any details about his rapport with the quilters and his professionalism. "I think Alan has found his right place right now." I squeezed Art's hand. "I also think he and Rachel will go far together."

Art beamed at my words, but he could take only so much

praise about his son. Grinning, he said, "Enough about the kids. Tell me about your meeting with Megan?"

I brushed the air to send his words away. "Cancelled. She's sick and will call me when she's feeling better."

"Too bad for her, and for you. *Our* day is almost two months away." He took my hand and held it between both of his.

"True. I'm not going to worry about it. We both need to focus on the upcoming days in our shops—and on the Square." I tried to sound casual and convince myself not to think about my meeting with Megan.

We finished before the lights dimmed, and headed home. Neither of us was prepared for the change in the weather since we'd arrived earlier. The cool air had us hurrying and Art didn't linger when I stepped inside.

Darn. I forgot to ask him about the invitations for the wedding. Tomorrow. I'd remember tomorrow.

6

After five years in the quilt shop I no longer panicked when tour buses arrived, even when there was more than one. Carla had a case of the jitters until the shoppers arrived and began to circulate through the store. Then she forgot about the number of visitors on the Square and helped one customer at a time.

When Carla mentioned we'd sold all the patterns by a talented designer, I knew it was time for me to spend an evening doing some extensive ordering. I didn't want to be out of pins, needles, rulers, or other standard items carried by every quilt shop. I wanted my shop to have everything quilters needed to complete their project. By the time I finished, Rachel had put Thomas to bed and joined me in the classroom.

"How was your day?" I asked, swiveling the chair to face her.

"Interesting, I think is the best word for it," Rachel responded pensively. "Gwen and I went through reservations for The Inn and every room is booked through New Year's. Hutch Hotels does a three-day New Year's holiday package at their big hotels. Cameron wants to try it here. It includes food and entertainment." Rachel shook her head.

"It would be nice for you and Alan to celebrate the New Year with Thomas."

"I don't think Thomas could stay awake 'til midnight," she said with a laugh, but immediately turned serious. "It seems that Thomas spends so much time at Sally's I wonder if he knows he has a home."

This had been a recurring guilt of Rachel's since we came to Wolf Creek. She needed to work and I had Quilts Galore to run. Our schedules pulled Thomas in many directions. His situation was similar to other children at Sally's, good or bad.

"I think Thomas is very secure that you—we, and others—love him and will keep him safe."

She bent forward to give me a hug. "Thank you."

To lighten the mood, I told her about Alan helping in the quilt shop that afternoon.

She laughed. "He told me he tried to use the register before entering the code and then he couldn't remember the code. He was going to walk away but didn't want the customers to think he was a thief."

"Wow," I said. "All he asked for was the code. He didn't tell me the rest."

Rachel asked about my meeting with Megan, and I explained that we'd postponed. "We'll meet when she's better." My voice carried an edge that surprised me. I forced myself to smile sheepishly. "Sorry. It's just that every day I look at the calendar and know that the wedding will be here sooner than we think. Your bridal magazines call it bridal anxiety."

She laughed. "Such a big word for what I call worry. Besides, why do they always focus on the bride? Don't grooms have jitters, too?"

I shrugged. "I guess we'll have to wait and find out."

Before I stopped working for the day, I checked for email confirmations of the orders I'd just placed. Speaking of worry, it seemed it was my nature to worry about shipments until the boxes were delivered to my door.

It had been a long day for us and for everyone on the Square. And with many more busy days ahead.

***

On Saturday morning, Carla was cheerful and laughingly assured me that she was ready for the arrival of the pair of tour buses arriving mid-morning. I started unpacking a shipment that arrived after hours yesterday and sent Carla off to restock several sections. Carla had proven herself to be a valuable employee, so I trusted her to follow my instructions.

Lucky for me she did.

I hadn't felt overwhelmed with shoppers in a long time, but that day I realized I'd depended on Liz and Rachel to be as efficient as I was with fabric cutting and check-out. Carla preferred the part of shopkeeping that involved talking with the quilters and hand-selling the fabric. That left me to cut and check-out. I hadn't felt that joyful in many days, either. Being around serious quilters reminded me of why I bought Quilts Galore in the first place. After the last shopper left, I told Carla I couldn't have gotten along without her help that day. Wanting her to know I appreciated her for a job well done, I asked if she'd like tomorrow off.

Carla frowned and scanned the shop—more or less in shambles. "But this place is such a mess after the day we had. Are you sure?"

I nodded. "Actually, putting things back in order and adding the new fabrics that came in is my chance to evaluate what I have and what I need." That was true, and I liked the solitary job of straightening up the shop after a nonstop day. "Don't worry, I'll be fine working alone."

Carla pulled a handwritten note out of her pocket and handed it to me. "I almost forgot. I put out all the sewing notions we have, but I wrote this list of items you may need to reorder. Seemed one woman after another needed a supply of pins and needles."

"Funny how that works, isn't it?" I remarked. "Thanks for keeping track. I can order right from your list."

Carla took a final look around. "Then I'll see you on Monday. Enjoy the day tomorrow."

"As I enjoyed today," I responded.

The bell jingled when she left.

I sent Art a text. Pza 2nite w T. Interested? I laughed at my attempt at my short cut text language.

I laughed even harder when Art replied. Coming w wine.

I closed out the register and waited for Art.

He arrived with both hands full, one for Thomas, the other with the wine. I knew it would be a bottle of my favorite flavor, DmZ Zodiac.

"Nana, look who's coming for dinner tonight?" He pulled my arm, so I bent to his level. "Will he play Cars with me?" he whispered, loud enough for Art to hear.

"I bet he will if you ask him." I looked at Art and he winked.

Art uncorked the wine while Thomas ran to his room to get his Cars game. Art had removed the magazines from the coffee table so they could build roadways and detours.

I handed Art a glass of wine and Thomas a glass of sparkling strawberry water. Art made a mock toast, thanking Thomas and me for inviting him, and the three of us clinked our glasses together.

I'm not sure who won the game, but when the oven timer buzzed to signal our pizza was done, Thomas was first to the table. Between mouthfuls, Art and I heard all about him having to use the detours for his car and then it had a flat tire, topped off by being held for two spins at a roadblock. "Terrible luck tonight, Nana."

"Maybe the pizza will make you feel better."

Thomas didn't wallow in his bad luck. He moved on to a constant stream of chatter about school and the new kids at Sally's. From there, he artfully told us about the toys he'd seen at The Toy Box next door, ending with a reminder that Christmas was coming.

"You've talked more than you've eaten, young man," I said, doing a poor imitation of a stern tone. "Finish up and then put your game away."

"But we were going to play another game, weren't we?" He turned to Art to support his plan.

Art knitted his forehead as if deep in thought. "Well, let's see. I'm thinking it's time for you to call it a day. We can play again another time."

Accepting his fate with only a low groan, Thomas swallowed his last bite. Then, he got away from the table and secured the game pieces in their box before scurrying down the hall.

Art's smile carried a note of nostalgia. "I remember Alan at that age, always trying to get me to play one more game or read one more story. Then later, I wondered if we'd make it through the rough spots."

"But you did," I said.

"I'm sure he'll manage with Thomas, too."

I wasn't in the mood for a trip down memory lane, and apparently Art wasn't, either. He got to his feet and pulled me into his arms. It gave me a wonderful reminder of why we were getting married.

"Kissing. Yuck!" Thomas stood in the doorway with a book in his hand. "Storytime, Nana."

Art pulled back and I let my arms drop to my side. "Pizza was great, but I need to get home."

"I'll follow you down to lock the door," I said. "You get ready for bed, Thomas. I'll be right back."

At the bottom of the stairs and again by the door, Art used his magic kisses to say good night.

Thomas was almost asleep by the time I got upstairs.

Rachel sent a text. Leave lite on.

It was our code that she would be late. I took the book out of Thomas' hands and gave him two extra kisses and told him we all loved him.

I put our few dishes in the dishwasher and stuffed the packaging from the pizza in the waste basket. Work that kept my hands busy while my mind raced between Quilts Galore and my wedding. The more I thought about all that needed to be done, the more I wondered if I'd have the energy for both.

7

With no tour buses scheduled for the next weekend, Carla and I were able to prepare for Black Friday and Small Business Saturday. In years past, I'd used scrap bags, smaller cuts of fabric mix-matched in clear plastic bags, and wanted to take the time to make them available again. They were inexpensive and became great quilter-to-quilter gifts. I benefitted from thinning out old stock and reducing the inventory. I pulled bolts of all colors in flower and geometric designs from the displays. They were bolts I considered outdated, and I put Carla to work cutting the fabric and creating the scrap bags.

Shortly after getting Carla started in the classroom, I received a call from Kim Mason, one of the new owners of the rental and maintenance company that took care of my house in Green Bay. Apparently, they were contacting all their clients as a way to introduce themselves and to assure their clients that their contracts with the company hadn't changed. I remembered getting a letter from the previous owners stating that same information, so I asked if there was some other reason for the call.

Getting right to the point, Kim said, "Two reasons, actually. First, the current renters in your home have submitted their thirty day notice. They're relocating for the husband's job."

"Do you have other renters interested in my house?"

"Not exactly, which gets to my other reason for calling," Kim said. "My husband and I like the house and the neighborhood. Would you consider selling?"

Kim mentioned a figure I thought was generous, but I wanted to consult with Jack before agreeing. "Give me twenty-four hours and I'll get back to you," I said.

Agreeable to that, we confirmed her contact information and ended the call.

I reached Jack right away, and after a whirlwind of calls, texts, and faxes I agreed to the offer. The Masons would come to Wolf Creek and meet with Jack and me for dinner on Wednesday evening.

The days flew by. Wednesday arrived almost before I'd chosen an outfit to wear. Jack and I got to Crossroads first, and while we waited, we reminisced about how quickly I'd bought Quilts Galore, despite his attempts to slow me down and create a formal business plan. No one could argue with that advice, but I wanted no part of it. I made up my mind about the quilt shop and with Jack's help, we concluded the sale that same day.

Now it seemed my house was selling about as fast as I'd made the decision to move to Wolf Creek. Kim and George were professional and engaging, and we completed our business transaction quickly. After dinner and dessert I had a contract, a closing date, and a check in hand. I saw a light on in Art's shop, and although I was eager to show Art that I'd cut my last tie to Green Bay, he was showing rings to a young couple, so I went home to tell Rachel instead.

"I liked that house," she said with a faraway look in her eye. "But I like it here better."

As Rachel and I chatted, I began to feel shaky, but managed to hide it until I was alone in my room. A flood of memories were like a video playing in my mind, each frame another memory of my life in that house with William. I left a few tears on my pillow that night.

***

Art called early the next morning to let me know he was passing on morning coffee. I went alone, though, and was happy to see Megan feeling much better. We arranged to meet that evening at 7:00 in the banquet room at The Inn. Liz was busy and passed on my invitation to join us.

"I'll let Rachel know we're coming," Megan said. "Bring a list, and we'll go through each item."

Walking back to Quilts Galore, I called Art to see if he was available and got his voice mail. I asked him to call when he could.

When Carla arrived, I told her it was time for her to learn the check-out procedures, which would help me as we got deeper into the holiday season. She was quick to learn, and efficient. She handled our steady stream of customers that day with only a few questions.

When Carla left for the day, I started to get increasingly nervous about my meeting with Megan.

Art didn't help. When he got me, he said he couldn't make the meeting or be part of the planning, but whatever I wanted…and on and on. He was acting as if arranging a wedding was my job, and he'd be fine with whatever I chose. This was upsetting and made me more nervous, so much so I ended up arriving at The Inn early, simply because I was too restless to stay home. I'd never had anticipated Art's odd attitude. I couldn't help but be disappointed that our special day wasn't going to be a blend of our ideas.

I was surprised to find the room unlocked. I stepped inside and found a single table covered in white linen. I put my swatch of Silver Bells fabric in the center of the table, immediately liking the contrast between the bright white covering and the dark blue. In my mind's eyes, I easily imagined a room filled with friends.

Megan came in all bouncy and happy, her cold apparently a thing of the past. She had a stack of notebooks—photo albums, I assumed—and a briefcase. When she approached, she touched the edge of the swatch.

"Oh, how perfect for your wedding." Pausing, she stared at it and then tapped the table. "Second marriages can be tricky, especially if one person wants a traditional wedding and the other wants something simpler and less fussy."

"Art and I agree we want a very simple, but obviously, nice wedding to enjoy with our friends."

"Got it." She opened the briefcase. In addition to her tablet, I noted lace samples, a wrinkled napkin, a necklace, and a mockup of an invitation. I could only guess at what other treasures were tucked in the corners. She had folders labeled with names for what I assumed were weddings. She set up her tablet on the table. It had a slide show of wedding images running, but then she rummaged in her handbag for a pen and pulled out an old-fashioned notebook.

"Traditional weddings around here are usually divided into four parts: the rehearsal, the wedding, the reception, and the gift opening. Each of those parts can be expanded to include a bachelor party, a bridal shower, an elaborate rehearsal, or anything else you'd like."

I quickly shook my head. "We want just the wedding and reception."

"No rehearsal?"

"We're adults, Megan. We know how to walk and where to stand."

She grinned and poised her pen above the paper. "Okay then, give me your thoughts for the wedding part."

"Divide this room in half." I held my arm out as a visual. "Two sets of chairs with a center aisle. No white carpet, maybe some flowers, but nothing elaborate. Art is handling the invitations and RSVPs will be sent to The Inn to coordinate with you."

Megan nodded and scribbled a note.

"After Thomas, Liz, and I walk to one end where Art and Alan will be standing, Richard will officiate." I paused. "At least I think he will. Art is supposed to ask him."

Megan held up a hand to stop me. "You're going to walk up a relatively bare aisle to Richard and the wedding party. With maybe a few flowers. Is that right?"

I nodded. "Yes, easy, nice."

Megan stood up and gestured around the room. "Then I can't be part of this wedding or have it connected to *Weddings at Wolf Creek Square*. You might as well go to the courthouse and have a party at a restaurant." She closed her notebook.

"Wait, Megan." I held my head in my hands and plunked

my elbows on the table. "I have no idea how to do what I imagined." Panic set in, nearly bringing me to tears. "I can't do this without your help. I don't know how to plan a wedding and I don't have the time. And Art's not onboard, either."

Megan touched my shoulder. "Let me suggest having the moving wall separate the wedding from the reception. Put simple bows—silver or blue or both—on the aisle chairs. Alternate sides, if you don't want every row to have one."

She walked to the opposite side of the room. "Your attendant—Liz—has preceded you, so she's here." Megan moved a chair to represent Liz and more chairs for Art and Alan. "Richard is back here." She turned toward me. "I have a set of arches that would make a nice backdrop for the wedding. Add a few flowers and greenery—maybe artificial trees on each side with small lights. Maybe pots of flowers at the base of the arches."

"Okay, that's enough. Let's not get carried away." I tried to stop her flow of ideas. "Remember, simple."

Megan joined me at the table. "Ceremony's over, now what?"

I tried to describe the reception room with the round tables decorated with vases of flowers. "Finger foods, easy to eat snacks. And drinks, sparkling water, wine, and coffee."

Megan continued to make notes. "I can coordinate with Melanie for the food. Do you want to approve her choices?"

"I've eaten at Crossroads and events they catered, so I know her items. They're all good. Can she make up a menu and I'll approve it?"

"And cakes? I'd recommend Cindy Baker, Steph's sister."

Plural, I noted. "*Cakes*, Megan? As in more than one?"

Megan nodded. "It's not so unusual. Nowadays, it's customary to have a bride's cake, a white cake, and then it's become popular to have a groom's cake, usually chocolate. One of each." Megan shrugged, apparently at a loss as to how to explain the reason to have more than one cake at a small wedding. Then she grinned. "For you, having the groom's cake might add a little fun to the day. Update it a bit."

Somehow, the image of the two cakes appealed. "Yes, I think you're right. I like the idea of updating. Okay, two cakes. I'll tell Art he'll have a cake of his own."

Megan visibly relaxed and let out a long exhale as she flopped back in a chair. "I don't think I've ever done a wedding this simple or with a less demanding bride."

"That's because it's more of a party than a wedding," I said. "Not a formal affair that makes everyone uncomfortable."

She grinned, which told me she understood. The knot in my stomach loosened as we went through her checklist. Megan based her business on making each couple's day uniquely theirs. Still, at times, she offered more, much more, than I wanted. She even suggested giving each one of the women guests a flower to hold. We finished with her list and she put her notebook in the briefcase. Before she closed the lid, I folded my fabric swatch and handed it to her.

"Thanks for agreeing to an evening appointment. I'm still doing some last-minute changes for weddings this month." Megan rolled her eyes. "I hope you don't change your mind as often as some of those younger women do."

"I'll let Art know we're all set. I should be thanking you for taking me seriously and making sense of my admittedly thin ideas. I didn't want an extravaganza like those in the bridal magazines. I know some families go into debt over limos and carriages and blocks of hotel rooms."

"I've seen that happen more than a few times, and it's sad when you get the feeling that the marriage won't last."

"By the way, Bev and Virgie are making Liz's and my dresses and a ring pillow for Thomas to carry." I reached for my purse and jacket. At that moment it dawned on me that I hadn't talked to Art about wedding bands for us. When I asked him about not wearing rings to show off his talents he said he'd worn a ring once and left it at that. Maybe it was time for us to talk more about those subjects we'd avoided earlier in our relationship.

"Thomas will make a nice addition to the ceremony. Most often the rings on the pillow are nondescript bands sewn onto the pillow." Megan was careful with her words, which surprised me. She was always chatty. "Let me put these ideas into a contract form and stop by the shop for you to review and sign, or make changes as needed."

"Soon? I'm getting nervous how quickly the days are passing and how little planning I—we—have done so far. We're a long way from ready."

"Busiest time of year on the Square, but oh, so much fun," Megan said. "I'll talk to Nora about flowers and vases. Stop by Rainbow Gardens soon and pick out the flowers and style of bouquets you want for you and Liz. Nora will take care of it. It's been fun watching her take more of an owner's role in the shop."

As we prepared to leave, Megan hefted the picture books into her arms and laughed. "I should have known we wouldn't need these."

"Are you going back to the office?" I asked. "Let me help you carry your things."

Megan's shoulders drooped. "I'd appreciate it. Guess I'm more tired than I thought."

We left The Inn and hurried to Heirlooms, where Megan's office was situated in one corner. With our quick walk and the warmth of autumn gone, it hit me that I needed to put away my light fall jacket and drag out a heavier one better suited for the chill in the air.

***

After another surprisingly busy day in Quilts Galore, I looked forward to the Wolf Creek Square Business Association meeting that evening. Art stopped by early, so we could walk the length of the Square to Crossroads together. Others were already there, and I was anticipating some questions about the wedding. I wasn't so nervous about the details now since I'd had a chance to talk to Megan and had a more solid wedding plan.

As always, we were greeted with hugs and handshakes, but maybe a little more enthusiastically now that virtually everyone on the Square knew Art and I were getting married. When Richard and Millie walked in, I leaned over to ask Art if he'd approached Richard to officiate the ceremony.

Apparently distracted, Art looked away, but I didn't see anyone in his line of vision. "Art?" I repeated.

"Yes, okay. I'll talk to him right now." He stepped over to Richard and a few seconds later, Richard nodded. I took that as a yes.

Art came back smiling, the task apparently done. "It's all set. Richard will officiate and have the license for us to sign."

"Good. I can check that off my list." If everything on my list took under a minute to complete, my stress level would be less. But why hadn't Art handled it before?

David tapped the podium with his knuckles to get the meeting underway. He still seemed like a newish manager of the Square, but he'd taken the job knowing he had big shoes to fill when he replaced Sarah. She had resigned and opened Heirlooms with Sadie. So far, so good. We all liked him. We quickly grabbed seats in the soft chairs.

"Glad to see so many members in attendance tonight," David said, and continued going through the routine agenda. He thanked us all for supporting the children's Halloween party and mentioned he'd received grateful calls from parents. David went on to announce the cancellation of a scheduled bus tour. Apparently, not enough shoppers signed up. There was a full-group groan. We all benefitted when the buses arrived.

Our spirits lifted though when David reminded us about the Harvest Festival Dance at the Community Center. This annual event was held for the whole community and one of the few town events not planned by the business association on the Square. David urged us all to go to show support for this dinner-dance that raised funds for town projects.

"This year's proceeds will be used to upgrade the community library," David said, adding that The Toy Box and BookMarks agreed to organize the raffles and hoped to raise funds to create a more comprehensive free learning center.

Meanwhile, my thoughts drifted off to trivial things, like what I'd wear to the Harvest Festival dance, which Art and I always attended. When David called on Georgia and Elliot to talk about Thanksgiving, I focused on their announcement.

Elliot stood and pulled Georgia up next to him. They went to the front of the room and Elliot casually draped his arm across Georgia's shoulders, as I'd seen him do many times.

"Georgia has the details, so listen closely," Elliot said. "There might be a test."

I enjoyed Elliot's teasing because it always brought on some laughter and added to the pleasant atmosphere that seemed to surround Georgia and Elliot.

Georgia grinned as she talked about their traditional co-op style Thanksgiving. "As usual, Elliot and I will fix the turkeys and you can sign up to bring whatever we need to complete the dinner."

Some things on the Square changed little, if at all. Georgia and Elliot's Thanksgiving at their farm was one of them. We all brought a dish to pass, and this year, Liz volunteered to keep the list of food. It was a holiday event to count on and saved us a lot of work when we were all preparing for Black Friday and the official launch of the holiday shopping season.

"This year, Zoe and Eli are showcasing his new label, so we'll have some new wine choices," Georgia added.

After Georgia and Elliot stepped away, David returned to the podium and asked if anyone else had something to add.

Art surprised me when he stood up. "Yes, I do." He grabbed my hand and led me to the front of the room.

"First of all, let me apologize to my wife-to-be." He squeezed my hand.

My first impulse was to pull away. Art knew I wasn't big on surprises. Not having even a hint at what he'd apologize for in front of this group made me nervous, shaky nervous.

"Marianna gave me one job to do for our wedding." He turned to look at me. "And I failed. So, that means we won't be mailing invitations. Sorry about that, but we ran out of time because I waited too long."

Anger was the first emotion to hit, and I fought back

the gathering tears. He'd taken on one job, but somehow, it hadn't been important enough to handle. I wanted to cancel the wedding right then, right there.

Art grinned, first at me, then to the group. "So, here it is, our personal invitation to join us on the Saturday after Christmas in the banquet room at The Inn. Marianna is working with Megan, so direct your questions to her. I know one thing for sure—it will be a party we'll all remember." Art pulled me into his arms and sealed the invitation with a kiss.

Kisses didn't soothe the wound. At that moment, I wanted no part of him. We left the podium and went back to our chairs, but I didn't sit. Without even looking Art's way, I grabbed my coat and left. I almost ran home. I wanted to hide from my friends, but mostly from Art. How could I have been so wrong about him?

I never turned the lights on in the apartment. I went directly to my room and added to my isolation by turning off my phone. Flat on my back on the bed, I folded my hands behind my head and asked *why*?

I lost track of time, but at some point, I heard a knock on my door. "Marianna? Can I come in?"

"Not tonight, honey. I'd rather be alone." I didn't want to get up, nor did I want to talk to anyone, not even Rachel.

"Uh, well, I guess I'll see you in the morning, then. Good night."

"Same to you." It was my standard answer to Rachel when we ended our day.

8

I avoided Rachel and Thomas, and didn't come out of my room until after they'd left. I had to hurry to get ready to open and it was nearly 10:00 when I unlocked the door. I groaned when I saw Carla coming across the Square with a to-go cup from B and B. No doubt she'd heard about Art's announcement, along with my uncharacteristic departure from last night's meeting.

"Morning, Marianna. We might see snowflakes today with that cold front passing through." She smiled pleasantly. "It sure makes me want to start decorating for Christmas."

"Then I'll let you take care of the window display for next month," I said. "I've lost my holiday spirit."

"Anything I can do to help?" Carla asked.

"Invite me to your house for Thanksgiving." I hadn't figured out what I was going to do about the annual event at Elliot and Georgia's farm.

"A friend and I have shared the holiday together for a few years now," Carla said. "It's sort of a tradition for the two of us. We eat and watch holiday movies and eat again. We make it a fun day for ourselves."

Realizing I'd made her uncomfortable, I quickly said, "Oh, I understand. Traditions are good."

Carla shifted her weight from one foot to the other. "Uh, about the shop…"

"Restock notions, books, patterns, whatever. I want the storeroom cabinets empty," I said with a heavy sigh. "Cut extra squares of fabric for the baskets. Stuff the shop. Make kits for easy projects to sew, extras can be stored in the classroom." As I spoke, I played with a small woven basket while I imagined Quilts Galore filled shoulder to shoulder with buyers.

I glanced down at the basket in my hands, and an idea hit me. "Let's make notion baskets. We'll put small items—needles, pins, a thimble, thread, and a square of fabric in a basket like this and tie a clear bag over it."

I turned to the register and pulled money from the drawer. "Go find some small containers to use. Maybe at Rainbow Gardens or Heirlooms. Small bowls will work, too." I shoved the cash into her hand. "Hurry back. I want to see how they will look."

"I'm gone." Carla got her coat and hat and left. She pulled the door closed so fast the bell did a double jingle.

If I'd been in her shoes, I'd have been happy for the chance to escape my company. I couldn't blame her.

While she was gone, I pulled bolts of fabric from various displays for her to use in the notion packs. On one of my trips back from putting bolts in the classroom, I saw Art standing inside by the door. I ignored him. I hadn't resolved what he had or hadn't done enough to talk to him.

"I'm sorry, Marianna." The rich voice I loved so much was tentative now, not a familiar tone for Art. "I should have told you before the meeting."

"Apparently, you don't care enough about *our* wedding to be involved at all. Is it the wedding you want no part of? Or is it me?"

He moved into the shop a few steps, but I moved back. "No, Art. I want you to leave."

Carla returned with bags from Rainbow Gardens and Heirlooms. With her eyes opened wide, she stammered out a greeting to Art, but kept walking until she was inside the classroom and closed the door.

Bless her.

When the bell jingled again and a trio of women entered, Art left and my heart went with him.

Carla came to the front of the shop and stood next to me. "You go have a look at my creations and I'll help these ladies." She gave me a warm smile and touched my arm. Woman to woman, Carla sensed I was dealing with a difficult situation. She never said as much, but I was sure she'd heard about Art's announcement and my response at B and B.

I tried to stay focused on her notion packs, which were colorful and eye-catching. I carried one to the register, hoping the shoppers would see it. Maybe it would generate some interest in a new item. Carla had found a whimsical elf and put the notions in the basket he was carrying. She matched a colored ribbon to his hat to tie the bag closed at the top.

The idea worked. The first woman to check out that day asked if there were others in the shop that she'd missed seeing.

"Well, no. But that's because Carla just started putting these together this morning. Let me see if she's got more ready." I waved Carla over and asked her to bring the other packs she'd assembled for the customer to see. She returned carrying four different containers.

The woman carefully looked over each one. "They would make a nice gift for our quilt guild Christmas party. We exchange gifts every year."

Carla held up one of her creations. "I'd like to get one, myself."

The shopper studied them for a few seconds. "Okay, I'll take three."

"These are what we have available now, so take your choice," Carla said eagerly.

The shopper chose three, and I put the remaining one next to the other on the counter. That kind of sale had me smiling. A simple idea of a quick and easy gift.

Carla clapped her hands together when the shopper left and the bell jingled. "Oh, this is so much fun. If I was your age, I'd consider opening a shop of my own."

"It is fun, isn't it?" I felt my mood shift and edge toward content. Still, being in the shop around the fabrics and quilts reminded me that I hadn't been at the sewing machine myself for a long time. Without over-thinking my idea, I turned to Carla. "I don't think we're going to be overly busy today, so I want you to mind the shop. I'm going to sew today and see if I can get more of that quilt done. Call me if you need help."

I disappeared into the alcove under the stairs.

***

The rhythm of the sewing machine relaxed me, which let me focus on my situation with Art. It reminded me of the many times during William's illness that sewing let me refocus on his needs at the moment, rather than on the loss I knew was coming.

I sewed and snipped and added one piece to the next building blocks and corners that would be assembled into a quilt top. When I needed to fill the bobbin thread of the sewing machine, I was forced to stop and take a rest. As the day ended and Carla left, I turned off the lights in the shop and continued sewing, using only the light on the machine. The darkness surrounded me like a cocoon.

Early on in my friendship with Art, I'd admired his persistence, whether it was entering a competition over and over until he received a high score from the judges or was one of the finalists. He'd been so persistent about the two of us being together one day. The kids would grow up, he'd said, and they did.

It had been nearly twenty-four hours since I'd left the meeting, and after turning off my phone, I'd set it aside, not wanting to deal with any attempts to reach out to me by either my friends on the Square or Art himself.

I was also a business owner with a responsibility to stay connected with customers and suppliers. So, when I turned on my phone, I was taken aback by the number of voice mails, emails, and texts.

As I scrolled through the lists, Art's name came up most often. His messages were short. ILU, I'm sorry, pls call. They'd started soon after he'd left the shop and continued all day.

I smiled, in spite of myself. Persistent, and I had to believe, sincere. We hadn't spent five years together without having deep feelings. Yes, I'd seen a new side of Art once wedding plans were underway, but that didn't mean he'd changed altogether.

Not yet ready to reply, though, I heard Rachel enter the shop. I quickly turned off my phone and slipped it into my apron pocket.

She quietly went up the stairs, whispering to Thomas, "Nana's busy tonight. You can see her in the morning."

"But..." was his objection.

Rachel cut him off with a firm, "No."

At that moment, I realized my response to Art's public show of disinterest in our wedding had spilled over to other people we cared about. Did our friends on the Square mind not receiving a written invitation? Was that even the point, though? On the other hand, was I becoming a diva bride?

I could rationalize and say our friends didn't care about receiving a written invite, but it wasn't only about that. Right from the start he'd shrugged off the wedding itself, as if he wanted nothing to do with the plans. So much for the give and take partner I thought I was getting.

None of this was Thomas' or Rachel's fault. I quickly turned off the sewing machine and hurried upstairs in time to give Thomas a hug before he fell asleep.

I reached out to squeeze Rachel's hand. "Good night to you, too. Life's spinning a little too fast for me right now. I need a couple of days to get control."

"By then the holidays will be here," she said, "and you'll be swamped with shoppers."

"Five years ago, I told you that if we didn't have shoppers—buyers—we'd have to move back to Green Bay."

Rachel chuckled. "I said it then and I'm saying it now, 'Bring on the shoppers. I'm not moving.'"

"We don't have a house in Green Bay anymore. No home to go back to."

She punched the air. "Yes!"

I gave her a quick hug and retreated to my room, thinking about my neighbors on the Square and how they'd welcomed me when I bought the quilt shop and become part of their community. I returned the favor when new shop owners arrived. We were all generous with our selling skills and promotional ideas.

Art was my first friend in the group. When I'd moved to the Square, he'd taken me to morning coffee and introduced me around. He came along with me day after day until I felt comfortable enough to go alone.

Our friendship had grown into a romance rather quickly, and memories of our first kiss would always be sweet. He'd not been shy with his feelings for me, but I was the one who thought of Alan and Rachel and Thomas. We both needed to be parents of teens and a baby. Maybe I'd used the kids as an excuse to keep Art at arm's length in the beginning while I adjusted to having a man in my life again. I fell asleep, thinking about the early days of our romance.

When the morning alarm sounded, I heard Rachel in the kitchen. The smell of fresh coffee pushed sleep aside and I got up to get dressed for the day. I waited to join Rachel in the kitchen until I heard Thomas' footsteps going past my door.

"Hi, guys." I made my voice light and happy.

"Hi, Nana. You slept late." He spooned in another mouthful of cereal.

"That I did, but now I'm ready for another day." I needed to tell myself that even if I didn't feel it.

Within minutes, they were ready to leave. I wouldn't see either of them until evening and that thought brought a quick jab of loneliness. I asked myself if I wanted to live alone. When I thought about Art, my immediate answer was no.

I waved at Rachel, but she hesitated at the door. "Call if you need to talk, Marianna. You've been listening to me for years, so maybe I can be a good listener for you now. I'll have my phone on all day."

I smiled to myself. Rachel had developed into such a wonderful, strong woman.

I went down to the shop shortly after Rachel left. On the Saturday before Thanksgiving my main customers were usually women visiting family, so I did a quick walk-through to make sure we were ready. The day before, Carla had filled the notion spinner, put sales bags by the register, and made sure the bolts of fabric were in the proper displays. As I unlocked the door, I saw her hurrying across the courtyard, arms loaded and shopping bags hanging from her arms. I opened the door and heard the happy sound of the bell.

Carla's cheeks were bright red from the morning cold, and probably from her rushed trips to Heirlooms and Rainbow Gardens to look for more containers. She passed me by and headed straight to the classroom where she unloaded her bags. "I spent more than I'd planned, but each container was cute or practical and we need both."

"Sounds good. Show me."

Full of sparkle, her eyes danced as she opened each bag filled with baskets and bowls. One bag had an assortment of ribbon ends. "Nora added those to tie the bags after I told her what we were doing. And at no charge."

Typical Nora. "That was kind of her."

"She's a beautiful lady," Carla said, nodding. "Have you seen the shop lately? She has Christmas displays in every corner."

I frowned. "I haven't been in any of the shops recently just to look around. Too busy. But taking time to browse the shops on the Square will be one of my New Year's resolutions."

"You still have plenty of time between now and the end of the year to visit." Carla began putting her notion packs together, tucking in fabric to fill empty corners. I stepped out to the shop when the bell jingled.

Uh, oh. Liz and Sarah weren't customers, but I could see from the look of their faces they were on a mission. I was sure of that.

"Good morning, you two," I said. "Something in the shop you'd like today?" I wanted to be on the offensive and had no intention of defending my actions.

The first person I needed to talk to was Art. In his last message, he promised he wouldn't barge into my shop during open hours. He implied he wouldn't bother me, but instead, he'd wait for me to call.

"Nothing from the shop, Marianna," Sarah said, taking a couple of steps toward me. "You're our friend and you seem to be in a bad spot."

"And because of that, you've come to...?"

They didn't have an opportunity to answer my question when a trio of women entered. From the look of them, they were three generations of women. I turned away to greet them. "Welcome to Quilts Galore. Something I can help you find?"

"We need to look around first, but yes, my granddaughter is getting married in the spring and I want to make a quilt for her," the grandmother said.

"Some of our spring fabrics have arrived and are over here." I walked them to the display of the new arrivals. Out of the corner of my eye I saw Sarah and Liz leave. Inside, I sighed in relief.

Carla chatted with the mother-daughter-grandmother group as she arranged her creations in strategic corners around the shop. Our day proceeded with customers coming and going, at times packing the store and making us shift into multitasking mode, but at other times it stood empty.

At closing time, Carla left as Alan slipped in and closed the door. "Hi, M A." He'd used his old abbreviation of my name. When he turned eighteen, he'd started using the full names of the shopkeepers on the Square. His own personal rite of passage.

"Rachel's not home yet."

Alan folded his arms across his chest. "I didn't come to see Rachel. I came to see you."

I gave him a pointed look, hoping I conveyed he was wasting his time.

"It's about Dad. I'm worried. He's not sleeping or eating. He doesn't seem to care if he sells any of his brooches or rings." His voice was hoarse when he added, "All he talks about is losing you."

"A little melodramatic, don't you think?"

Alan shrugged. "Easy to say, but I've never seen Dad happier than he's been these last few weeks. Designs poured out of him so fast he couldn't make them all."

I smiled in spite of myself. But on the other hand, by not doing anything to plan our wedding he had all kinds of time.

"Dad's been giving me pointers to make my necklaces better. He sent me links to some competitions he's come across."

"That's nice. Maybe you should give one a try."

"Marianna, I'm telling you he whistled, he sang…he was happy all the time."

I waited for him to finish. "I see you are concerned, Alan, but this is between Art and me. It doesn't involve you."

"I understand that," he argued, "but he's my dad and I want to help him. At least try."

"And you've done your best." My voice, devoid of all emotion, even displeased me. I wasn't the person I wanted to be at that moment, but I believed only Art and I could sort out our troubles and break through this impasse.

"Sounds like that's my signal to leave," Alan said, his tone glum. He turned on his heel and left without another word.

Alan was seeing a side to me he'd not witnessed before. But so be it.

Alone in the shop, I had a decision to make. Art had done his part. He'd texted, called, and showed up here. I was holding out. Was I going to be adult enough to cross the divide?

Yes.

I loved Art. There was no second guessing that feeling and there would be no future for us if I reacted this strongly to every misstep or disagreement we would have as a married couple.

Cowardly me, instead of calling, I sent a text. I luv U.

His reply was immediate. Bench date, dress warm.

I hurried upstairs and grabbed a winter scarf and hat, along with my heaviest fall jacket. I pulled on gloves on the way to the door. When I opened it, I saw Art waiting for me. He stepped away from the bench and held out both arms. I walked into them like my life depended on it. Maybe it did.

He wrapped me tight and whispered, "I love you."

That was all I needed to hear. Deep down inside I knew

we would bridge this gap and any that would arise in the future.

"I'm sorry, Marianna. For making you think I wasn't interested in our wedding plans, or that I'd brushed off your expectations. Someday, we'll look back on this time and laugh."

"It's nothing to laugh at," I shot back.

"All things like this get funny with age."

I bristled at his flippant remark, which sounded strange coming on the heels of what had seemed like a heartfelt apology. I struggled to put that aside.

We sat on the bench and I told him about Alan's visit and that Sarah and Liz had come by that morning. Not wanting to hash out what happened, although I needed an explanation, I asked him about the ordinary things we shared, like his designs. That led to sharing other things.

We talked until the stars sparkled in the dark about his focus on his jewelry and my plan to give Quilts Galore a full makeover in January. We added ideas for us to keep a balance with our businesses and life. He told me again that the loss of his first wife left him reeling and how long it had taken him to recover. Art credited the people of Wolf Creek Square for helping him recover. We shared that experience, because I had become isolated with my sewing after William died.

Alan had had a hard time losing his mother, and that wasn't unlike Rachel's mother rejecting her. All in all, the four of us had gone through events that had taken a toll but hadn't broken our spirits. That's why our happiness was so special.

We were both shivering by the time we made our plans to meet for morning coffee. "I'll be on the bench waiting," he said, and gave me a kiss before going home.

It was more than a kiss, though. It carried a promise of tomorrows we'd travel together.

9

On Thanksgiving, Art and I left mid-morning to drive the short distance to Elliot and Georgia's home for a day of feasting, friendship, and a dose of football and a few raffles. Mother Nature added her Thanksgiving surprise that morning by leaving a layer of frost on everything, a reminder winter was approaching. Just like my wedding day.

When Art pulled into their driveway, a number of cars had already parked in a neat row near the house. We took the next space in keeping with the pattern. Inside, the guests flowed from one room to the next, sharing good wishes and some talking football.

We mingled around, sipping coffee and eating bite-sized pieces of muffins and scones. In small groups, we walked out to the barn to look at the horses Elliot and Georgia had acquired. Eli showed us his vineyard and talked about the special grapes he was growing for wine.

Returning to the house, Art and I helped Elliot and Georgia and several others spread the buffet on the kitchen counters. When the turkeys were ready to carve, Elliot whistled sharply to get everyone's attention.

"Gather 'round," he said. "It's time to give thanks for another prosperous year, for family and friends, new and old, and for health and happiness."

Art stood next to me and squeezed my hand.

It was a fun day filled with good-natured teasing about the upcoming wedding—and talk of holiday sales. I didn't offer specifics, but I didn't mind saying that if sales trends held and I had a good December, then it would end up being my best year since I'd opened Quilts Galore. Sales had already passed my projected goals for the year.

"Mine, too," Zoe said. "I've been thrilled with the numbers Square Spirits is showing."

Zoe and I were among those enjoying some coffee around the large kitchen table in Georgia and Elliot's kitchen. We'd finished with the food and dishes, relaxing in the last few minutes of the day.

"I don't have exact numbers yet," Nora said, "but the wedding business has put Rainbow Gardens over our goal."

Nora and Megan did a happy high-five.

"Most brides want exotic flowers this year and, boy, are they expensive," Megan added. "I know one wedding that won't be elaborate or exotic, but that's all I'll say about it." She flashed a sly smile.

"Uh oh, the game must be over," Georgia said as a group of men came into the kitchen from the lower level.

Nathan and Lily were the first to pack up their kids and leave, followed by Rachel and Alan taking Thomas with them.

Soon, we were left with a chorus of "thanks" and "see you tomorrow" and "drive carefully" filling the air. Art and I were among the last to leave and followed the stream of cars back to the Square like we'd planned a parade. I reached across the console to take Art's hand. A few minutes of connection to him was all I needed to end a wonderful day.

Art parked behind Art&Son and walked me to the back door of Quilts Galore. "I can't believe it's only a month until the wedding. Are you getting excited?" I asked. I'd tried not to let the passing days derail me—us—but when I thought of the holiday shopping days ahead and Christmas to celebrate before our wedding, I needed to stop and take a deep breath.

"I'll be too busy selling jewelry to think about the wedding."

I yanked my hand away. "Good for you."

Art pulled me to him. "No, no. That didn't come out the way I meant it. Sure, I'm focused on holiday sales, which have to be big to make my year a success. But c'mon, Marianna, you know being with you has been my dream for years. Each day that passes, my dream is becoming real."

"Okay," I said. I couldn't quite catch his point about sales being more important than us.

"But I can't let this wonderful dream of ours overshadow the reality of making jewelry and running the shop."

I snorted a laugh. "Sorry. I'm overreacting to everything lately. These last few weeks have been a rollercoaster and I guess it's caught up with me." Suddenly, I yawned. "See? I had a great day, but I need sleep."

"All of us do," Art said, cupping my cheek in his gloved hand. "We have to be sharp for tomorrow and Small Business Saturday, and Sundays will be busier now, too."

I gave him a quick kiss. "Okay, Art. A friendly wager. I bet I sell more than you do this weekend."

"You're on. What does the winner get?"

"Dinner and more kisses." I waved and hurried inside, where the warmth of the shop was a welcome change from the cold November night.

***

Black Friday was truly black, at least as far as customers and sales went. It came as a complete surprise to me that I could have easily managed without Carla. I offered her a chance to go home, but it seemed she was eager to see how the legendary shopping day played out.

Everything changed the next day. Bright and early on Small Business Saturday Liz arrived with large coffees for Carla and me. She was spending her day with me at Quilts Galore. It had become a Thanksgiving weekend tradition for us.

"I'm planning to be so busy I'll need the extra caffeine to keep me going," Carla said, taking sips of her coffee.

"That's the spirit," I said with a laugh. "Keep those good thoughts up."

Eventually, the customers started coming in steadily, not in big numbers early on, but good enough to lift my spirits.

Carla's attention to detail and knowing what we had in stock made it easier for Liz and me to help the customers as traffic picked up throughout the day. When we were getting low on an item, Carla was prompt to fill the space, and she efficiently checked out customers. I'd told Carla and Liz about my bet with Art, so as often as I could I updated my sales numbers. He did the same. Our bet added another element of fun to the day. He was never far from my thoughts.

Pat came by with box lunches for all of us, compliments of the business association. I recalled how surprised I was my first year on the Square when Sarah came by with lunch. Pat waved and headed to the next shop. Another Wolf Creek Square tradition.

We needed to stagger our lunch breaks, but not wanting to miss any shoppers we mostly stayed in the shop. At the end of the day, we each had half a lunch left. I offered my bright red apple and the brownie to Carla to take home. She accepted and put them in her box.

"It's been such a fun day for me. I can't wait to get home and call my friend so I can describe all the shoppers." She pointed to Liz. "And to tell her about you." Off she went, with the bell jingling to punctuate the end of Small Business Saturday.

"Why don't you and Art join us for dinner?" Liz suggested.

I shook my head. "I want to relax tonight, but thank you for thinking of us. I'm looking at dismantling the front window display early in the morning and during breaks between shoppers."

"You'd think they'd be all shopped out by now," Liz said, laughing. She knew shoppers were born to shop, anywhere, anytime.

"I'll take the day as it comes," I said. "I'm done making predictions."

Liz gave me a hug and left.

Rachel and Thomas arrived soon after. Thomas stuck out his stomach to show off his full belly. "Mom and Alan and me went to Creekside for burgers and I ate all of mine and fries. And…a soda," he added in a whisper. Soda drinks were an extra-special treat for him, so he always spoke of them in hushed tones.

"Good to see you were able to get out for dinner with Alan and Thomas tonight," I said, giving Rachel a pointed look. Her schedule had been packed even fuller than Alan's, so he ended up taking charge of Thomas many evenings and delivering him to me around bedtime.

"Me, too. It's clear we need more hotel help. Gwen's going to talk to Cameron after New Year's. The entire Inn is booked for the New Year's special, and with so many guests we'll have a full staff working.

"Seems like The Inn has proven itself," I said. "Cameron was right to build here."

Rachel nodded, and then turned her attention to Thomas, who came to me for a hug.

"Night, Nana." He smiled. "I made a jingle. 'Night, Nana… 'Night Nana." We could hear him sing all the way up the stairs.

Rachel hung back. "It's not my business, but are you and Art okay? It seemed so at Georgia's." She was still holding Thomas' coat and fidgeted with the string on the hood. "Alan told me he came to talk to you."

"He was worried about his dad, which made me realize my stubborn refusal to respond to Art's calls and texts was affecting more people than Art and me."

In a soft voice, Rachel said, "Until I came along, Art was the one steady person in Alan's life. I'm sure he doesn't like seeing him hurting."

"Art's action—or non-action, I should say—took me by surprise. It seemed like he didn't really care about the wedding. I overreacted. We've talked about it."

"I'm glad to hear that. Besides, you're too smart to let a guy like Art get away." She laughed as she hurried up the steps to be with Thomas.

***

The month ended on a high note for me and Quilts Galore.

After adding up the receipts for Black Friday and Small Business Saturday, and comparing them to Art's sales, the quilt shop won. It was a small margin, but good enough for me to crow a little.

We were at Crossroads for C and D when we compared sales.

Art looked at my tally and frowned. "Wait a minute, here. You had Liz helping that day. So three people were selling. I only had Alan, so that means I get to add one-third more to my total."

I flopped back in the chair. "Oh, please…is the loser changing the rules now that he's lost the wager?"

"Nah, I don't cheat." He made a pouty face.

"So when do I get my prize?" I asked.

Grinning, he said, "I guess you'll have to wait until after the wedding."

I responded to that idea with a pout of my own.

December
10

I started the final month of the year holding my phone in front of me to shoot photos of Thomas tossing snowballs in the air. I'd add them to the already considerable collection I started five years ago. The first of December surprised us with three inches of snow. That was the first surprise, and watching my grandson play always brought me great joy.

I wasn't prepared for the second surprise. Beverly called just as I'd unlocked the door to begin the day. She started with profuse apologies. But for what?

"We've looked everywhere, Marianna, but Virgie and I can't get our hands on any of the dark blue fabric you want. It seems to be the color-of-choice this winter, and all the distributors tell us the fabric is backordered, with no firm date for availability."

I worked with fabric. I knew about print runs and color trends. Fashion designers created annual color pallets to keep customers buying the new clothes.

I was at a loss of what to say, so I left it at, "What do you suggest?"

"Maybe you could find something you'd like at Styles," Beverly said, her voice tentative. "Mimi and Jessica always have a good selection of holiday clothes."

"You mentioned the blue, but what about the silver? If we can get that, I'll change the blue to another color." I thought longingly of the Silver Bells fabric in my room upstairs.

Beverly sighed. "The silver is available, but in other tones, not that rich color you wanted."

My voice was flat when I said, "I just don't know what to say. I'll call you back. I need to talk with Liz."

"Virgie and I are so sorry, Marianna."

When I ended the call, I stood in silence and stared out at nothing. Were the stars aligned *against* my choices for our wedding?

Seeing Carla's quizzical expression, I explained what happened. As usual, Carla was sympathetic for a few minutes and then turned on her action switch. She instantly made the search for my new wedding outfit seem like a treasure hunt. "But not red…anything but red," she said. She turned away quickly, as if she'd given out a piece of private information.

Now I was puzzled. "Why not red?"

She backtracked her steps to come closer. "It's after Christmas, and by then everyone will be tired of green and red."

I rolled my eyes. She was right. Even I'd be tired of red by the end of the month. "Holiday burnout. I agree."

I refocused on the day in front of me. Enough of my personal problems. "What are your plans for the window, Carla?"

"Been meaning to ask you about the kinds of displays you've done the last couple of years. I remember them being attractive, but I don't recall the small accents."

Since I'd only done five it was easy to remember the general themes. My photos of the windows could supply the details. I told Carla she'd find boxes of decorations and a worn out tree downstairs. "Have a look and see what's there you might be able to use."

Carla nodded with a "got it," and she was on her way to the lower level of the building I used for storage. We had limited storage areas in the shop and nowhere near enough closet space upstairs, so after Rachel and I moved in, I'd had Charlie Crawford put together storage shelves and garment closets in the basement.

I didn't anticipate many early morning customers, so

I called Liz, then Art, then Styles. Like Carla, all were surprised by the news, but Liz's response was a mystery to me. She, a trendy dresser and very particular about her look, immediately said she'd go to Styles and find something I'd like. *Huh?* Liz brushed the situation aside like it didn't matter much what we wore. Now that was strange.

Art tried to be sympathetic, but I had a feeling what I wore wasn't all that important to him. He'd drag out his good charcoal gray suit and look great. "You could wear a burlap bag, for all I care, my love," he said.

His rich laughter eased some of my tension. I signed off with, "Big help you are."

At least Jessica was more sympathetic. "Bev is here doing fittings for alterations and told us about the problem with the fabric. I've put aside three dresses for you and two for Liz. Stop by and have a look when you get a chance."

"Can you stay open a few minutes after hours today if Liz is available?"

Jessica laughed. "Of course, Marianna. Don't worry. We'll try to find something you'll fall in love with. And something for Liz. We'll help make it happen."

I clicked off and redialed Liz. My call went to voice mail. While I was leaving my message, the first customer arrived. I took a breath and switched off my concerns. "Good morning. Is there something special I can help you find today?"

"Have you ever given an undone quilt as a gift—a wedding gift?"

My immediate response would have been no, but seeing the stress on the woman's face I softened my answer. "I think it would depend on my relationship to the couple."

"The bride is the woman's best friend."

That filled in the blanks. "Then I don't see a problem with that kind of unique gift."

Relief crossed her face. "I was hoping you'd say that." She opened her purse and withdrew the pattern for the Double Wedding Ring design. "I think four or six rings as a wall hanging would best suit the couple."

"Do you have colors in mind?" I asked.

The woman raised her open hands in a helpless gesture. "No, not really. Maybe you could help me choose colors that go together."

I smiled. "I can do that. It's always fun to pick colors that blend. We need to avoid any large prints, though, because the pieces are small and the design would be lost."

The woman frowned. "Then would you go ahead and pick the fabrics? I'm afraid of making a mistake." She sighed. "I want her to be happy with it."

She followed me as I wandered through the shop picking bolts of soft green, pale peach, a lemon yellow and one of powder blue. I asked the customer about my choices as I made them, and she nodded more than once. One of the easier sales I made. When we took the bolts to the cutting table, I decided that we needed lavender in the selection of colors I'd chosen. I stepped aside and returned to the cutting table with the bolt of soft purple that would bring the design alive. "Do you like this combination because now is the time to change it if you don't."

She touched the bolts. "They're beautiful together, so soft and comforting."

I cut the yardage as the pattern required and added a small flowered white on ecru fabric for the center of the rings. "If I was making this for myself, I'd choose these same colors."

"I'll let you know if my friend likes it."

"Have her stop in and show us the finished project." I laughed to myself, thinking how much I'd love to have the quilt I'd just designed.

She left with a Quilts Galore shopping bag and one of the Food and Fabric coupons I was giving out in December to be used in January. Melanie thought a coupon for Crossroads, added to those the other shopkeepers were giving out, was a way to encourage a post-holiday winter visit to the Square.

Carla was smiling when she returned from the basement with her arms filled. "I'm on overload. I wanted to use everything I saw, but then the window would look like we were having a close-out sale."

She was joking, but her words gave me an idea. "That's something to think about for January." I glanced around the shop. "I'm planning a whole new look for the shop—a real update."

"Wow. Now that's an undertaking."

I pointed to the far wall. "Some of those quilts have been hanging more than a year now."

Carla laughed. "Let me focus on Christmas first."

She was right, of course. We had the busiest month ahead—not to mention my wedding. "Okay, a conversation for another day. Let's clear out what's in the front window today. It's a slow day, so we can get a lot of little jobs done."

Working together, we dismantled the window display, but when two women entered the shop I left Carla to start the new display, one to her liking.

"Would you like help or are you just browsing?" I asked the shoppers.

"Browsing first, then questions," one said.

I went to the cutting table and began the forever job of making small cuts for either the baskets or the scrap bags. Pondering my ideas for the new look for the shop gave me something to think about other than my dress— my nonexistent dress—and all the other details for the wedding going through my mind.

"This is a very nice shop," the older of the two women said as she fingered one of the bolts I'd just cut. "Do you hold classes?"

"Up to now, no," I said. "I'm alone in the shop much of the time, so it's not possible to offer classes."

"My friend's being coy," the other woman said. "It happens that our husbands are meeting at The Inn for a three-day corporate retreat in February. Some of those attending are bringing their wives or husbands along. We're actually on a mission to look for some things the women might like to do when their husbands are in meetings. Someone else will have to come up with ideas for the tag-along husbands."

"We noticed a classroom and thought a one-day project would be fun," the older woman said. "We think we'll have six women altogether. If we rotated two at a time, each person would get one full day of attention."

"Are you thinking that sewing would be their only activity?" I asked.

"We were also thinking about flower arranging, or maybe a book discussion at the bookstore," the other woman said. "The owner of Square Spirits volunteered to organize a short class on the basics of gemstones—or one on wine. Maybe some of the men would like that."

Holding classes in February, when the days could get long, would be fun. "Okay, since the shop isn't as busy in the winter, we could have a class long enough to finish a small item. Or, almost complete it."

I told them about the baby blankets the women shopkeepers on the Square had made. We'd enjoyed the time together as much as the sewing.

"Here's my contact information," the older woman said, handing me her card. "If it's all right with you, I'll send an email in January and we can coordinate from there."

That was fine with me, and they were happy to sign up for my newsletter. They left with my business card and a coupon. The bell gave me a happy feeling.

Unlike other shops on the Square, it wasn't unusual for my sales to drop off in December. Most women were too busy with holiday preparations to think about sewing. Books and patterns and gift certificates generated steady—and quickly handled—sales.

As the days passed, Carla continued to take charge of unpacking new stock and keeping the store looking fully stocked with fresh supplies. Not being so busy myself gave my mind time to wander.

And wander it did, meandering around and landing on the wedding plans and my dress. I tried to focus on finishing the quilt top I was working on before the end of the month, but each time Art sent a text telling me he'd made another sale, I wondered if he'd surpass my sales and win the bet for this month.

One afternoon, near closing time, Liz rushed in carrying two books. "Hot off the press—just in time. I stopped at Heirlooms and Sarah signed these for you."

I took the books from her hand. "Oh, Liz, how exciting

for her—and for you. And now for the Square. She's been working on this history for a long time."

"Matt wants her to have a book signing," Liz said, "but it could be tricky for her to be away from Heirlooms on a Saturday or Sunday."

Seemed like an easily solved problem. "Why don't you help Sadie at the register for those few hours?"

"I told you I'd help here on weekends."

I swept my arm in a gesture that encompassed the entire store. "Can't you see all the customers? We've had so many that Carla was able to start and finish the front window in one day and dust every inch of the place."

She waved my words into the air. "Okay, I get it. I like working with you, but if I'm needed elsewhere, then that's where I'll go."

"Spoken like the Liz I've known all my life." It was true. No one had a spirit quite like hers. "Before I forget, can you go to Styles after closing time? We need dresses."

Liz checked the time on her phone and frowned. "I can, but not for too long."

She was meeting her son and his family for dinner and celebrating their Christmas early. Then the kids were off to visit the other side of the family. Jack and Liz enjoyed spending time with Todd and his wife, Brooke, and they adored their granddaughter, Andrea, but they sometimes had to share the holidays with her family.

"I haven't even given much thought to gifts this year." I touched my forehead. "My mind has been on other things."

"Can't imagine what," Liz quipped as she rushed out as fast as she'd rushed in.

***

On our way to Styles at the end of the day, Liz and I passed The Toy Box. As I glanced at the window display, my eye caught a set of construction trucks Thomas would love. I kept walking, but sent Skylar a quick text telling her to hold a set for me.

Finding a gift for a little boy I loved so much lightened

my heart. Otherwise, I'd have arrived at Styles feeling down about having to search for a dress when I'd designed one that was perfect for me. A great gift for my grandson or not, I wasn't in the best mood. I took a deep breath and exhaled with a loud sigh. My way of steeling myself to look at dresses I never wanted in the first place.

"Come on, Marianna," Liz said, hurrying me along, but sensing my lack of enthusiasm. "You've always loved the clothes in Styles. Jessica and Mimi have kept us both looking good for years."

"That's not the point. It's the whole ordeal of trying on dresses and making a final choice."

"It won't be that hard to decide. You'll either like them or you won't." Her voice carried a hint of exasperation.

I crossed my arms over my chest. "I've already decided I won't."

Liz's pointed look wasn't subtle. "Are you *trying* to be a difficult bride? No one expected the fabric to be back-ordered. It's time for you to accept Plan B." Her words were sharp, so unlike the lady I'd called my friend for decades.

Not wanting to shoot back a remark I'd regret, I let myself be distracted by the festive window display in BookMarks. It was bright with greenery and bows of gold ribbon arranged around a display of paperback editions of holiday stories for both adults and children. "Thomas needs a few books to go with his trucks," I commented, knowing I was buying time.

Liz was having none of it. "Enough, Marianna. We're on our way to choose dresses. For your wedding. Remember? You're getting married to the man of your dreams. It's not about the dress. And we're not out for a stroll to do your holiday shopping."

Defeated, with what energy I had left rapidly draining away, I held up my hands defensively and stepped to the side to open up space between us. "Okay, okay, I get it."

We passed Heirlooms, where Sadie was locking up, and then Liz opened the door to Styles. Soft instrumental holiday songs were playing in the background. After greeting us in her typical warm way, Jessica turned to me. "I'm sorry you have to find another dress, but…"

"I know," I interjected before she could go on.

"But, like I was saying, I've already picked out three outfits that I think you'll like. And I've set aside a couple for Liz, too." She gestured for us to follow her to the back of the shop toward the dressing rooms.

Liz and Jessica exchanged a look that communicated something I could see wasn't meant for me to know. Their little frowns and tightly pursed lips were nearly identical. Were they worried I'd become unhinged or something? Maybe so. I was certainly acting glum and difficult.

When we got to the back of the shop, Jessica pointed to her hold rack and cheerfully said, "Okay, Marianna, let's have a look."

I was stunned—and not in a good way. The colors, red, green, and gold were perfect for Christmas. But not for my wedding. They were skimpy cocktail dresses that would be great on a younger woman, but not for someone my age. I shook my head. "No, no, no. I don't like any of them." I sighed.

Jessica turned back to the rack. "I chose these two for Liz." She held up a black and silver pant suit and a flowing floor-length chiffon dress that might have been okay for a mother-of-the-bride, but not for a matron of honor. Besides, the fabric was deep green. It reminded me of a dark dense forest, not a fun, upbeat winter wedding.

I threw up my hands. "No, no. Those aren't right."

"Why don't you walk around the shop," Jessica said, a nervous jitter in her voice. "Maybe you'll see something you like."

Liz touched my arm. "I need to leave. Todd and his family are at Crossroads with Jack." She gave me a hug.

I stood there alone surrounded by a store filled with beautiful clothes, on the verge of tears. I heard the door open and the bell jingle, and in the next minute Art was standing next to me.

"Thought you might need a little support." He gave my hand an affectionate squeeze. "Especially if you don't find a dress you like."

"Turns out I wasn't joking about burlap. I may be reduced

99

to that yet."

"But to me, you're beautiful no matter what you wear."

I swatted the air in front of me. "Oh, quit with the clichés. I'm not in the mood." I walked past him and approached Jessica. "Thanks for staying open later. I'm not sure what I'm going to do to solve this problem. I'm running out of time."

Jessica frowned. "Sorry you didn't find anything appealing. I know you'll look stunning in your blue dress." She clamped her hand over her mouth and quickly turned away.

Art distracted me when he cupped my elbow and led me out the door.

We walked to "our" bench in front of Quilts Galore. I rubbed my upper arms through my jacket. Art put his arm around me and squeezed my shoulder before we sat. "Pretty soon we'll need warmer coats to sit on the bench."

Something Jessica said seemed odd and I couldn't put my finger on it. "Did you hear Jessica mention my dress?"

Art seemed to fumble for words. "Uh, well...I don't know. I think she said you'd have looked beautiful in your blue dress."

I nodded. "I guess I heard her wrong." I took a deep breath and said, "Enough about me and the dress. Tell me about your customers, new ones and those that come back every year."

"I think I'm up to that challenge," he said, grinning.

Was that gloating I heard in his voice? I wouldn't admit it, but the way he talked he planned to win the sales wager for the month. We'd have to see about that.

***

Before heading out the next morning I noticed the writing on the calendar. A reminder. 14 days. I didn't want that ruining my morning, so I closed the door behind me and hurried to B and B for coffee. The conversation was all about the record number of shoppers on the Square, so spirits were high. On my way home, I stopped at

BookMarks and bought the two books for Thomas I'd seen in the window. Millie and Claire were also in high spirits. They were having a banner month due to their two-for-one sale and BookMarks partnering with The Toy Shop for toy-book combinations.

Skylar had received my message and put the set of trucks aside and would hold them for me until closer to Christmas, so I was assured Thomas wouldn't find it. Buying toys for Thomas put me in a more grateful mood and I put aside the dress issue for another day. I sent a thank you text to Jessica for staying open and for choosing possibilities for me to wear. Still, I was confused. Jessica had put effort into choosing dresses that weren't my style at all.

That was puzzling. I'd been shopping at Styles for years and Jessica often set aside a skirt or a pantsuit or a sweater she thought was perfect for me. About 90% of the time, she was right. Her comment about my blue dress passed through my mind now and again throughout the day. Obviously, Art and I hadn't heard her remark the same way.

When I got down to what was in front of me in the moment, I began to think about gifts for Art, Rachel, and Alan. I needed Alan's help with Art's gift because it was related to his jewelry. With both Art and Alan making an increasing number of pieces, their kiln was too small. I texted Alan and asked him to stop by when he had a free moment. I needed technical advice.

Alan got back to me quickly. Free time a premium, but for u I will find some.

A few minutes later, Alan was in my shop, staring at me with eyes getting larger by the second as I told him what I wanted to get Art.

Finally, he said, "Dad's going to love it, but this equipment isn't cheap."

"Let me worry about that, Alan. Just stand here and make sure I'm ordering the right one." Alan guided me through the particulars of different models of kilns until we settled on the Metrics DLX 3517. A couple of minutes later, an email confirmation arrived.

"Not a word about this," I said. "Not even a little hint. I don't want anything to spoil the surprise."

"Not a chance," Alan said, grinning.

"So, do you have gift ideas for Rachel?" I asked. "I don't want to give her clothes or any of those standard gifts."

"You mean like socks?" He laughed, and his cheeks got a little more color in them. "I'm giving her jewelry. I'm planning to do a special series of necklaces and call it The Rachel Collection."

Just the sound of the name made my heart beat a little faster. Talk about romantic. "Oh, Alan, that's a wonderful idea. She'll love it. And that gives me an idea. I know Reed Crawford makes wooden toys and special boxes. Maybe he still has time to make a jewelry box for her. Why don't I call him and see."

Alan's face lit up. "Special boxes? Maybe I'll see what he can do for the collection."

"I'll bet he'd jump at the chance to design a unique box just for your series." I was on a roll. I still needed a gift for Alan, but he might be embarrassed if asked him directly about his wildest dream gift. No, Rachel could help me with that.

When I brought up Alan's gift later that evening she was brimming over with ideas, some of which were kind of frivolous and fun, like a new car, or even a new suit, as if I'd know what kind of suit he'd want. But Rachel mentioned one that intrigued me.

Rachel's forehead wrinkled up in thought. "Alan mentioned a PR conference that a large firm, Kline & Bryce, is hosting in Chicago in January. They're bringing in three speakers from New York, who have worked with big companies, you know, the Fortune 500. Alan said he could learn a lot from a conference like that. New techniques to use in campaigns promoting The Inn and the Square."

"Perfect. I'll look it up online and see if I can get him a reservation."

By the time Art and I had C and D at Crossroads that evening, Alan was registered and his hotel room secured.

Other things were on my mind, but I wanted to focus on our wedding.

"Do you realize we'll be married in less than fourteen days...about 13 now."

Art grinned. "I do, but that means a wedding, and what's happening with your dress?"

He'd hit a sore spot, but I tried not to let my irritation show when I said, "I have a blue dress I bought years ago. Liz will choose something from her closet, too. She hasn't decided yet."

Putting his hand over mine, he said, "A wedding isn't about clothes, it's about two people pledging their love for each other and making a commitment in front of family and friends." When he held my gaze, all I saw was love in his eyes. "And after we say "I do," I'll be ready for a party with the people who are more like family than our actual families."

I kept his words uppermost in my mind as I got ready for bed later that night. He was right, of course. But I'd have been lying to myself if I claimed I wasn't harboring some disappointment about my dress.

***

The next week passed, some days slowly, others more quickly when Quilts Galore was filled with shoppers. The rush in my shop was over about the time the last-minute gift buyers flooded to the Square. I could handle the run on gift certificates I was likely to have, so I gave Carla an early bonus, a gift certificate for the shop. I also asked her if she'd like to continue working for me after the first of the year, and she eagerly said yes. She'd enjoyed her job and fit into the crowd of owners and employees on the Square. I knew she was pleased to be invited to the wedding.

As the holiday neared and the bell on my door jingled less often, I enjoyed the quiet hours and being alone with my bolts of fabric—and my thoughts. I reflected on the five years I'd owned Quilts Galore. I never regretted buying the shop and moving to the Square. Meeting Art had made the move uniquely special.

I thought about that move again when I looked out my window and saw Alan trudging across the Square with a backpack slung over his shoulder. A pair of tied sneakers hung from one of the cinch hooks on the side. Later that evening, I asked Rachel where Alan was going with the duffel.

At first she looked puzzled, but then shook her head. "I almost forgot. He's moving some of his things to Reed and Nolan's place. Making room for you in Art's apartment."

"Of course. We talked about that weeks ago." It made perfect sense. When Rachel and Alan got married, Alan would move into my place. "Not everybody's housing arrangement could be as simple as ours. I like the way Art turned his apartment into a real home." Even more so than I had with mine. Most of my energy had gone into my shop.

As Christmas neared, my quiet days were interrupted with calls from Megan. We went over all the arrangements from flowers to food. What a roller coaster it could be. She'd tell me that certain foods weren't available for the reception. Then Melanie would call to offer alternatives. I kept swallowing back disappointment about this or that detail, but somehow I knew that Melanie and Megan would see to it we'd have really good food for the reception.

Thomas had been getting excited about his serious role as ring bearer, one of the few embellishments I wanted. So far, no mishap had changed that plan.

One evening, Rachel confided that the women of the Square had put their heads together to figure out what she'd dubbed, "a non-shower bridal bash." Since most of the women I'd invite to a shower were immersed in their holiday shopkeeping, including me, it seemed the women wanted to host a brunch for me at Crossroads in January. I smiled to myself. That idea had Rachel and Liz's fingerprints all over it. They'd known I'd prefer an event planned around the gift of friendship, rather than being about other kinds of gifts Art and I didn't need. It wasn't as if we were just starting our own household and needed a toaster or coffee pot. Far from it.

The days counted down fast, and soon Rachel, Thomas, and I celebrated the holiday on Christmas Eve, with Art and Alan joining us for a late supper and gift exchange. We'd started that tradition a few years back.

We let Thomas open all of his gifts first since it was way past his normal bedtime when we finished supper. He hooped and hollered and paper scattered as he barreled through his packages. When I suggested he slow down, he gave me a funny grin and said, "But Nana, it's Christmas."

Who was I to argue?

We'd all relied on Skylar for his gifts and she'd made sure Thomas received a full set of construction trucks, loaders and cranes with all the battery run bells and whistles. By the time we'd helped assemble everything, his construction site reminded me of the excitement on the Square the previous year when Cameron Hutch, owner of Hutch Hotels, came to town and built an addition to The Inn.

Rachel gave Thomas some time to play, so he didn't put up too much of a fuss when she hustled him off to bed. We all got extra hugs and thank-yous as he made the rounds.

When it came time for the adults, we went with the one-gift-at-a-time tradition, with old-fashioned deference to "ladies first." I insisted Rachel open Alan's gift first, and then the one from Art and me.

Her eyes misted when she saw the necklace he'd made for her. She held it up and we could see he'd fashioned a butterfly by encasing wings of malachite stones in silver. "Oh, it's so beautiful, Alan."

"Like you," Alan said, adding that a butterfly grows from a plain-colored worm into a beautiful free adult. "Just like you did. That's the first necklace in a collection, by the way."

"Really," she said. "That's wonderful."

"I've already named it The Rachel Collection."

Rachel went from misty to tearful real fast. Art and I smiled at each other when Rachel threw her arms around Alan and gave him a quick kiss.

Art had insisted on sharing the cost of the jewelry box

for her. Reed had hand-crafted a velvet lined box, which I'd wanted, but Art had asked Reed to make the cover out of small pieces of different woods. If I looked with squinted eyes, I could see some of the wooden pieces looked like butterflies. Rachel seemed to run out of words when she opened the package.

Then it was Alan's turn. The PR conference coordinator had sent the thick conference packet to me, which gave me time to put it in an oversized box and wrap it with Christmas fabric that hadn't sold in the shop.

Rachel laughed at my creative wrapping. "I remember we used fabric to wrap the gifts our first Christmas together."

A memory of that first Christmas flashed in my mind. We'd had many firsts that year, for me as a stand-in parent for an almost grown teenager, and for Rachel, adjusting to be the mother of an infant son.

By the time Alan had gotten through all the packaging and found the folder, I had my camera ready to catch the look of excitement in his eyes when he picked up the conference brochure. Other than, "Wow," he was speechless. I knew I'd chosen the perfect gift.

Rachel and Alan were soon deep in reading the conference brochure, so Art and I started our gift exchange without them.

"You first," I insisted, handing him his package.

He shook the small box. "Good things come in small boxes, Marianna. Like you asking me to marry you." He winked.

I twisted the ring on my finger. He'd made it, and it came in one of his signature boxes, so yes, I had reason to like small packages. "Go ahead, Art, don't be shy. Rip that wrapping right off."

He smiled slyly and tore the last of the paper from the box. I shot a picture when he lifted the lid. I wanted to have pictures of Art and later, when our evening was winding down, I'd ask Rachel to take a couple shots of us together.

He unfolded the computer printout of the order confirmation for the kiln. I'd never seen Art at a loss for words so when he mimicked Alan's "wow," I laughed.

"A kiln? Really?" he asked. "Had a little help picking this out?"

"Alan knew exactly what you needed. It'll be delivered the day after tomorrow. At least that's when it's scheduled."

"Then I won't have to share with Alan anymore."

"That's not the spirit of the holiday." I bent forward to give him a kiss. It was the important half of the gift.

Art put the paper in his shirt pocket. "With this mess I might lose it." He reached forward and handed me a small box from under the tree. "For you."

I carefully undid the bow and lifted the cover of a blue Art&Son box. An intricate Christmas tree brooch was nestled in the white packing.

"It's the first of my new series I decided to call 'Holidays.' Well, actually it's the last month, but you're the first to have one. I'll begin selling them in January, one for each month."

I looked more closely at the brooch, which included tiny ornaments and candles on the tree. "So much detail, Art. It's breathtaking."

"I used a technique called cloisonné. Enamel and fine wires are combined to make the design. Someday I'll show you how it's done and you can make one of your own."

He described his concept for all twelve months. "I've thought about changing the packaging from my signature blue box to seasonal colors, but Alan nixed the idea. The blue box is really a trademark, so I need to stick with it."

I nodded. "I'm with Alan on this one. You can change your pieces, but not your branding."

Art laughed and held out his hand. "You are so smart. That's why I love you." He led me to the front window that looked out on the Square with its wreaths and Christmas bells. This year, David and his assistant Pat had chosen to weave white fairy lights around all the shrubs and the street lamps. They'd put up an arch at one end with a banner reading, "Welcome to Wolf Creek Square." The Square's Christmas tree sat at the opposite end.

I looked behind me and saw Alan and Rachel in the kitchen, clearing away the last of the glasses and plates of snacks we'd put out. They were laughing and talking, so easy with each other, like two people who'd known each other a long time. A little more than five years to be exact.

"Oh, Art, this has been such a special Christmas for all of us. We're becoming a family for real. It's truly the best gift." I intertwined my fingers with his.

"Each year will only get better after Saturday." He kissed me again. "I suppose you better send Alan home soon."

I laughed. "They're adults. They'll get the message when you leave."

I went downstairs with Art, and after some kisses full of passion and promise, I went back upstairs and said a quick goodnight to the kids before I headed toward my room.

"Marianna," Alan called out. "I don't know how to thank you and Dad. This is a terrific gift. So on target for where I am in my life."

"You're welcome, Alan. I only want you to use all your talents." I grinned. "Well, and take care of Rachel and Thomas, too."

Alan chuckled. "Now that's an easy promise to make. You know how much I love 'em both." He extended his arms out to the side. "They're my whole world."

I waved as I shut the door to my room. Yes, this Christmas had surpassed others, but I knew, deep in my heart, we'd have more wonderful years to come.

11

I'd originally thought of closing Quilts Galore for my wedding day, but Liz called to ask what I'd do until late afternoon with the wedding set for 6:00. "Going to Green Bay to the spa for a day of pampering?" she teased. "I wish you'd let me plan something to pass the time. We could have had our hair done or maybe manicures."

"Not my style." My tone sounded flat, even to me. "Besides, I'm still longing for my dress." That came out like a teenager's whine.

Ignoring the dress remark, Liz asked in a more serious tone again how I planned to pass the time.

"I don't know…wander around the shop, cut some fabric, sew on the quilt, think about the January sales. Like I said, I don't know."

"So, you're keeping the doors open for customers? *Today?*"

"I hope a few come around. Maybe that would help calm my nerves." That was a bit of a lie. I wasn't all that nervous. My moodiness wasn't about that.

Liz sighed. "Okay, you keep busy and I'll come by around 4:00 to help you dress."

"I know how to dress myself. Been doing it for a long time." The edge in my voice hadn't softened.

"Okay, then, I'll help you *get ready.* Is that better? From what I hear, that's part of my job. You know me, I'm no slacker. Especially not today." Odd, Liz sounded more cheerful than I did.

I smiled in spite of myself. "Okay, if you insist. Actually,

109

give me a call before you come. I think I'll stay open until around 2:00." I thought of the dress I wanted but couldn't have, and my mind drifted to the one in my closet. At least it was blue. Not the blue I wanted, but still, I'd be comfortable in it.

I clicked off the call and started to make a sign for the door— Closing at 2:00 for wedding. At the last minute, I added a caret before "wedding," and wrote "my" above the line. It wasn't just any old wedding, after all. Art and I had been waiting for years for this day. I frowned. I guess that's why it seemed like I ought to be able to have the dress I wanted. And Jack officiating.

My shop was empty until noon when a customer rushed in for thread and needles. Then a steady stream of shoppers occupied my time, most of them surprised when they read my sign and were taken aback that I'd opened at all. On my wedding day? It was hard to explain, so I laughed it off as if I was just a bit eccentric. But at 2:00, I locked the door and turned off the lights.

Having a shower and putting on my simple make-up took no more than forty-five minutes. I put a robe over my slip, suddenly at a loss about what to do next. The time dragged, which allowed my anxiety to spike. I'd checked in with Megan yesterday and two days before that, but somehow, I needed reassurance again. I made the call, but all I got was voice mail…with her cheerful message of "wedding today, will call back later." Okay, her words reminded me that she'd handled the details.

Before Christmas, Rachel had cleaned out the piles of magazines that tended to accumulate, so all I had around were my quilting magazines, but I knew they wouldn't hold my interest. I dialed Art, but got his voicemail. I imagined he'd turned his phone off. I ended the call without leaving a message.

As the time approached for Liz's arrival I took another look at the dress from my closet and groaned. I'd started a real pout when Liz called and interrupted. "Unlock the door, Marianna. We're here to help you get ready."

We? "Whose we?"

Silence. She'd already disconnected.

I went downstairs and to the front where Megan was waving her arms, wearing a big smile. Virgie and Bev, who carried a garment bag, stood behind her. Liz was grinning from ear to ear. When I opened the door they shouted, "Surprise!"

Liz all but pushed me up the stairs. I kept turning around to ask questions, but she kept saying, "In due time."

Standing in the living room, I watched Bev unzip the bag...and saw my dress. *My dress!* The one I had dreamed about.

"How?" I was too dazed to form a more coherent sentence.

"You didn't really believe we'd disappoint you, did you?" Bev had a sly smile on her face.

I blinked back tears, unable to keep my eyes off the dress, *my* dress. "I...I can't believe this is happening."

Virgie took charge and took the blue dress off the hanger. "Try this on. Now. We can do some minor alterations if needed.

I took off my robe and tossed it on the couch. I pulled the dress over my head and smoothed it down. A perfect fit, and the jacket, too. It was as if they had been made to fit only me. Well, it *was* made just for me. I immediately went to my room to have a look in the full-length mirror. From the front, the back, and both sides, the colors and workmanship needed no changing.

I stepped into my heels and went back to the group. "I can't believe this is happening."

"You said that earlier," Liz said dryly, but her eyes sparkled.

Virgie looked at her watch. "So, go change back into your regular clothes. Bev and I will drop your dress off at The Inn on our way home. We have to go and change into our fancy clothes, too. Liz's dress is already waiting there." Virgie's smile reflected mine.

Megan stood to the side, her phone to her ear. She mouthed "Art" and pointed to the phone. So, did that mean he was in on this scheme, too?

I gave Virgie and Bev a good-bye hug and when Megan

finished her call, I wrapped my arms around her. It was a struggle, but I managed to keep the tears at bay. I didn't want to be redoing my make-up, little that there was. No tear-streaked face, at least at the start of the ceremony.

Liz took my hand. "I think you and I should head to The Inn. We can check out the wedding space and the reception room before the guests start arriving."

I cupped my face in my hands. "It's really happening, isn't it, my friend? I'm marrying Art Carlson today."

Liz's eyes misted when she said, "I couldn't be happier for you. You and that fabulous man of yours have waited a long time for this day."

I smiled. "Rachel calls Art a good man. And she's lucky to have Alan, who learned from the best."

We gathered our coats and Liz insisted on carrying the tote with my makeup bag and shoes. "It's my job to assist you today, so no argument."

"Yes, ma'am." I locked the front door of the shop and handed her the keys. We walked arm in arm across the courtyard to The Inn, to my wedding.

Ashley met us at the entrance of the banquet room. "Have a quick look and then I'll lock the door until the reception begins. Cindy will be delivering the cakes soon. Nora is on her way with more flowers."

Liz followed me into the room. The tables, the flowers, the decorations were as I had pictured them in October when I saw the Silver Bells fabric. Someone had put a table off to the side for gifts, I presumed, as a decorated box had CARDS written on it in block lettering. The DJ had set his equipment in the corner.

"You like it?" Ashley's voice carried a note of apprehension.

"It's beautiful. More than I dreamed. Is Megan here?"

"Not at the moment. She's taking care of a few last minute details."

Liz touched my arm. "Time to get dressed. Ashley has us using Gwen's office tonight. It's the only space available in this booked-up place."

"I'll come and get you when the guests are seated,"

Ashley said, closing and locking the door behind her when she left.

We were dressed in a matter of minutes. Liz looked perfect in her cocktail length dress in shimmering blue silk. "You look fabulous," I said, "as usual."

As we stood fussing with sleeves and admiring our dresses, I waited—expected—Liz to give me an explanation for what had taken place. Everyone knew I had a dress, except me. When none came, I finally said, "How long have you known our dresses would be ready?"

Liz responded with a dismissive wave. "Oh, I don't know. Maybe it was from the very beginning when we decided to shake this party up a bit." She laughed. "But that's water under the bridge."

"Wait, wait, what do you mean?"

Liz put her hands on my shoulders. "Okay, let me put it this way. From the moment you announced your engagement to this man of your dreams, a wonderful guy who completely adores you, you minimized everything about the wedding." Her exaggerated eye roll got a laugh out of me. "All we heard was 'small, simple, no fuss'. Well, a few of us decided not to pay attention. But if we'd told you, you'd have argued. You can be pretty obstinate, you know."

Oh, she was so right. I realized that with a little internal jolt. "And Art was in on it?"

"We twisted his arm, my friend. He took a little convincing."

Laughing, I said, "I'm sure he worried I'd call the whole thing off."

"Well, you didn't." Liz grabbed my hand. "We'd never have let it get that far. We had a few bad moments over those invitations. So, let's go enjoy your day. *Your* special day."

Ashley knocked on the door, then stuck her head inside. "It's time, Marianna."

We went to gather with the rest of the wedding party. Rachel was there with Thomas, holding the ring pillow he would carry. Nora handed Liz her bouquet and then she gave me mine. Every flower was the deepest blue and the small silver Baby's Breath filled the spaces between the flowers. Three streamers of silver ribbon hung from the bouquet.

I took a breath and looked to the far end of the aisle, where Richard stood facing the guests. Art and Alan stood to his left. I immediately noticed the three of them wore ties made to match the blue fabric of my dress.

Thomas turned to give me a big smile. "Mom says I have to do a good job tonight, Nana."

I squeezed his shoulder. "I'm positive you will."

The music started. Liz whispered in Thomas' ear that it was time for him to walk down the aisle to Art. He held the ring pillow as if he was carrying his favorite toy. Liz followed Thomas and then it was time for me to go towards the man I loved.

I stepped out with the first chord of Mendelssohn's "Wedding March." Knowing it came from *A Midsummer's Night Dream* made it extra special. There I was, in the middle of my very own mid-winter dream. The distance to Art seemed so far, but my heart was hurrying to be with him. It seemed like mere seconds later, I took Art's hand and Richard began the ceremony, which we'd embellished a little to make it uniquely ours. We'd realized soon after we'd met that we started with friendship, right along with the magic of attraction. It was our friendship that had given us the patience to wait until the time was right, until *our time* to be together had come.

Since Art had made our rings, he slipped a wedding band on my finger, but I didn't have one for him. Once again, Liz knew the plan and pressed Art's ring into my palm so I could put it on his finger.

And then, the ceremony was all I had dreamed about for years. Simple, yes, but oh, so meaningful. When we shared our kiss, both of us had happy tears in our eyes.

Richard asked us to turn toward our guests, our friends. "We've witnessed the marriage of Art and Marianna," he said, "but after we congratulate them, I ask that you stay right where you are. We have yet another surprise for Marianna."

I was lightheaded from knowing that our moment had

truly arrived and the buzz of voices from various parts of the room echoed in my ears.

"So, as they say," Richard continued, "let's congratulate Marianna and Art Carlson."

The room erupted with applause and a few cheers.

Then I saw Rachel.

She stood at the back of the room dressed in a floor-length ivory dress with a red sash at her waist and a ring of Baby's Breath in her hair. She carried a single red rose.

I was so distracted by the sight of her I didn't notice Liz alongside me.

She lifted my bouquet out of my hands. "I'll keep this safe for you, Marianna. But it's time for you to carry this one." She handed me a bouquet made of red and ivory miniature roses with a red streamer.

"She asked for you to be her matron-of-honor," Liz whispered, pressing a ring into my hand. "This is Alan's ring."

Feeling blindsided, completely confused, I managed to wave at Rachel, who grinned and waved back. Astonished, I looked at Art standing next to me. His grin covered his face. He pointed back at Alan, who stared at Rachel like they were the only two people in the room.

Art's squeezed my hand and brought me back to the reality of what was happening.

"You knew all about this? My dress, the odd stories about glitches and not sending invitations? And now this? Our kids' wedding?"

"I did." He put his arms around me and whispered in my ear. "We all knew. Liz and some of the other women wanted you to have a wedding as special as you are. The kids had been planning a winter wedding anyway, but they didn't say anything because they didn't want to overshadow our day."

"But we could have…"

Art stepped back and touched his fingers to my lips. "Marianna, none of it matters. These two weddings fell into place with the help of a whole bunch of people."

"You're right." I took in the scene unfolding in front of me. Rachel was still in the back, grinning. The guests were milling about talking and laughing. Suddenly, I was laughing, too. "Well, we've been married all of five minutes, but I guess we each have a job to do."

I turned back and blew a kiss to Rachel and then moved into my place to Richard's right. Art and Alan stood opposite me.

When the "Wedding March" started for the second time I watched Rachel approach with her arm laced through Jack's left arm. Thomas was hanging onto Jack's right hand.

Jack...of course. He wouldn't have missed this day.

I took a deep breath. We were becoming a family.

Jack left Rachel in front of Richard and guided Thomas off to the side. Richard appeared thrilled to repeat the ceremony in his upbeat, light-hearted tone.

Rachel and Alan, who were beaming enough to light a room, had prepared their own vows. They'd met as teenagers and had grown up to become members of Wolf Creek Square.

I stood next to Richard, still reeling from the surprise, but with enough presence of mind to long for my camera— or at least my phone. Then I spotted a young woman holding a camera with a couple of others slung over her shoulder. I'd seen her as a photographer at other weddings and remembered Megan had added a photographer to the contract. I hadn't even noticed her when Art and I stood before Richard.

Midway through the ceremony, Rachel turned to me for Alan's ring. Her face was all love and happiness. A tear slipped down her cheek, but I reached up to whisk it away. I wouldn't let even a happy tear mess her makeup.

Within minutes, Richard said, "Please congratulate Rachel and Alan Carlson." Again, the room erupted with claps and whistles.

Rachel turned and embraced me in a tight hug. "Two Spencer women became two Carlson women on the same day. Did we surprise you?"

I gave her a long-suffering look. "Now, what do you think? Art filled me in, but I want the full story in detail later."

"We'll have plenty of time for that," Rachel said with a beaming smile.

We were soon engulfed by our friends, most of them proud of what part they'd had in the surprise. We had no need for a formal reception line, so Ashley soon pulled back the dividing wall to reveal the beauty of the reception room. Vases of blue and red flowers were centerpieces on each table. Confetti in silver and red were sprinkled around the vases on my Silver Bells fabric.

In the corner, I saw the cakes and pulled Art's hand to go see them. There were two—mine with blue flowers and Rachel's with red. Cindy had written 'Father and Son' on the chocolate cake.

I turned to Art. "I'm floating on air. My feet have to hit the floor soon, or I might disappear!"

"This is just the beginning, Marianna, my wife." He chuckled. "I've waited a long time to say that."

The evening took on a party atmosphere when toast after toast was given, along with a lot of teasing. I watch Alan's face turn bright red a few times. Art and I made the rounds of the tables, greeting people we'd known for a long time and considered our friends. Zoe, stunning in a flowing velvet dress, was quite the sensation on the dance floor with Eli. Millie and Richard were a close second. Clayton and Megan danced most of the night, with lots of partner switching. By the end of the evening, Rachel and I had danced with Jack and Richard, Nolan and Reed had stayed, along with Skylar and Ashley, although Ash had to leave often and tend to business. It was great to see that Stephanie and Jessica and Mimi made sure Carla enjoyed herself. All the most important people in our life, Art's and mine, were in the same room.

After midnight, when our friends began to leave, Cameron, with Sarah by his side, came to join us at our table. Seeing Sarah so happy made me wonder if another wedding could be coming up one day soon. "You have a suite here tonight, on the house," Cameron said. "Room service will deliver breakfast at 9:00."

"So that was your surprise," I said to Art, who refused to

answer where we'd spend our wedding night. We'd already decided we'd treat ourselves to a trip during the winter in a warmer climate. Plenty of people could cover Quilts Galore for a week or two in February.

"Rachel and Alan have a room down the hall from you."

Ashley stepped forward and crouched down next to me. "That reminds me, Rachel prepared an overnight bag for you. I put it in the room earlier."

We thanked Cameron and Ashley and then I went to find Rachel, who was with some of the younger people still gathered around one of the tables. She and Alan were standing hand-in-hand, ready to leave.

"You really pulled one over on me," I said with a laugh. "I wondered why you seemed so casual about when you were getting married."

"What a fun ruse," she whispered, "although I didn't like seeing you upset about your dress."

I smoothed my hand over the beautiful fabric. "All is forgiven. What a beautiful day." I squeezed her arm. "Speaking of beautiful, look at you, Rachel. Your dress, your hair, your flowers…you're a stunning bride."

Rachel and I both had tears in our eyes. We seemed to have run out of words.

Alan and Rachel left, but Art and I stayed at the table until Elliot and Georgia finished dancing to the last song of the evening. They joined us when the music ended. "We don't get out dancing much anymore. Been a great party, and the surprise was worth all the secrets." With hugs and a handshake, they left.

Art asked the DJ to play one more song for us. He chose a slow instrumental version of the old, but classic, "The Way You Look Tonight." We were alone on the dance floor, a perfect ending to our day.

As we left, Megan came alongside us to let us know that the gifts would be secure until morning. "Melanie has the cake tops in the freezer." With a wistful smile she said, "I hope your wedding filled all of your expectations."

It had—and more.

12

Room service arrived promptly at 9:00. Wearing the robe Rachel had given me on Christmas morning, I opened the door to let the waiter roll the cart in. His cheery "Good morning" made me smile.

"Marianna?" Art called from the bathroom. "Someone at the door?"

"Room service with breakfast, but he's gone. You can come out now."

A few minutes later, there was another knock.

"Grand Central Station," Art deadpanned.

I answered the door to find Alan and Rachel and their room service cart. "We thought it might be fun to share breakfast as a finale to the weddings," Rachel said.

Alan didn't wait for me to reply, but pushed their cart into our room.

Unlike me, Rachel and Alan had dressed and were ready to go for the day and gift opening.

I turned and gave Art a helpless look when he came out of the bedroom, looking surprised. He'd thrown on sweats and a T-shirt.

"Another surprise...how about that?" I said in a voice I was sure he'd read as sarcasm.

"Hi, Dad. We're here to share breakfast. We didn't have much chance to talk last night."

"Come in," Art said, waving them in, "or rather come farther in, since you've already rolled the cart inside." He winked at me. "We're all family, but it seems from here on out, we won't be sharing too many more breakfasts."

Nice, I thought, Art making it fun to be together that morning.

Rachel removed the warmers over the plates—four identical breakfasts.

"Must have been easy for the chef," I said, laughing.

"Ashley told me they'd never done a wedding breakfast before today. Guess we are the guinea pigs for this service."

Rachel grabbed a bacon slice as Alan pushed the carts over to the table near the window.

"This is great," Alan said, plucking a muffin from the basket and adding it to his plate of eggs and bacon, and sausage.

"Strawberries in December. What a treat." I savored my first bite of the fruit.

Our conversation left food and reverted to the weddings and the reception. I learned that Art had schemed with Rachel and Alan as early as October to surprise me, and they'd schemed with Liz and Megan to make sure it all went without a hitch. It also explained why we couldn't have invitations.

I didn't know what to say. On the one hand, I felt bad Art had to pretend to let me down, but on the other, I was the one who had to deal with a lot of pre-wedding anxiety.

"We almost abandoned the surprise and told you what we were doing, but Art said no. He was willing to be the fall guy." Rachel popped a grape into her mouth.

I rested back in my chair. "I'm not big on surprises, so you took a big risk. But it turned out to be a wonderful surprise. We'll laugh about it for years to come."

"If I'd been too involved in the wedding plans," Art said, "I'd have had too much trouble keeping you in the dark. I was bound to slip up."

I reached across the table and covered his hand with mine. "I understand, but I have to admit you didn't seem like yourself at all. That's what threw me off."

"I hope I'm forgiven," Art said.

"You are," I said. "No worries there. It was all beautiful."

"I guess you realize by now I didn't really move in with Reed and Nolan," Alan said with a laugh in his voice. "I had to bring those two in on our secret."

"Funny, I thought of that when I saw Rachel in her dress. It all started falling into place. You covered everything."

"It's almost funny when you think about it," Art said, looking at me. "We can finish moving you in to my place and now Alan can take his things out of his room and stop pretending to go to Reed and Nolan's at night."

"And Thomas finally has his own room," Rachel said.

"My old room could be a design studio for you, Dad," Alan said.

"Uh, maybe you'd better keep Alan's bed, though," Rachel said, "so Thomas has a place in your house."

Art and I hooted. "We get it...maybe Thomas could have a sleepover now and then."

Alan and Rachel both turned pink fast. "Well, and we work such long hours," Alan added.

I nodded. I got it. "Isn't it terrific all four of us can stay on the Square, at least for now?"

A knock on the door interrupted us before anyone could respond.

"I'll get it," Alan said, quickly getting to his feet and going to the door. He opened the door wide and found Megan. "Hi, come in. We're finishing breakfast."

She stepped into the room and closed the door. "Morning, everyone. I hope you think our surprises were worth the frustration, Marianna."

"Coffee, Megan?" With an amused grin, Art held up the carafe that had come on the cart. "No Clayton? Or maybe Nora would like to stop by."

I got a kick out of Art's humor, but it seemed to be lost on Megan, who thanked him but said she had to be on her way.

"I'm just here to check on all the arrangements," Megan said, "and return Marianna's keys. Liz let us put all your gifts and cards upstairs at Quilts Galore. She has your clothes and make-up."

I stood and gave her a hug. "Thanks for all you did to make our day special." I gave her a pointed look. "Including all the surprises...I guess. I have to admit, keeping me in the dark meant I wasn't always a happy bride-to-be."

"I know, I know. I'm not sure I'll agree to that kind of scheme ever again. I'm glad it all turned out so well." She waved and hurried away.

Rachel got up and said she and Alan needed to pick up Thomas from Sally, who had agreed to take him overnight, and head home—to the quilt shop home—to get ready to open the gifts.

Rachel hugged Art. "Thanks for everything. I'm glad you are my father-in-law."

The kids took off hand-in-hand, but Art and I took our time leaving The Inn. I still hadn't put all the pieces of the surprise together, and while we enjoyed another cup of coffee, Art started his story at the beginning, the day I reserved the banquet room.

I told him that I was getting suspicious—not to mention resentful—when he refused to help me plan the wedding. "It was like I was marrying myself. Not the most romantic idea."

"That was tough. But like I said, I was so sure I'd spoil the surprise."

"If I decide I ever want to surprise anyone, I'll tell you about it first." I leaned across the table and gave him a kiss.

We dressed and gathered our things, then walked the full length of the Square to Quilts Galore. A dusting of snow made the courtyard look clean and new, like our life.

The door to the quilt shop was open and the bell jingling announced our arrival. Thomas' voice was the first I heard. He ran down the stairs. "Nana, it's Christmas again upstairs. There are packages all over." He spread his arms wide.

"Well, let's go see." We let him go up first and followed at a slower pace.

"Mom said you won't be living here anymore...and... and I can have my own room. Isn't that cool?"

"Pretty neat, I'd say." We'd reached the door to the apartment. Thomas had been right. Gifts were scattered around the room.

"We started separating the cards, thinking we all should be here for the gifts." Rachel took my hand and had me sit on the loveseat. She moved a package so Art could sit next to me. "These are the ones addressed to you."

She handed Art a bundle secured with a rubber band. "We've put ours away to open later."

"Packages, Mom." Thomas pulled on her arm.

Alan and Rachel sat on the floor with Thomas between them. Alan had his phone ready to take pictures.

"Open that silver one, Alan." Art pointed to the one near Rachel's leg.

Alan let Thomas help with the wrapping, but when I saw the name on the outside of the box I burst out laughing.

"The woman at the store said every young couple should get a toaster as a wedding gift." Art lifted his shoulders in concession.

"How funny," I said. "We need a new toaster. The one we're using only works on one side."

Art looked at me.

"What can I say?" I said. "I only toast one slice for myself."

Rachel made sure I opened the next package. I recognized the fabric immediately, and the enclosed Double Wedding Ring pattern.

"Liz and I wanted to make that for you and Art, but we knew we'd never have the time to get it done. So, Liz asked one of her friends to play the shopper and have you pick out the fabric you liked. But now that Liz is done with Sarah's books, she has time to put it together."

"I remember that woman," I said. "She had a whole song and dance about trusting me to pick the colors I'd like. And so I did. Trust Liz to come up with a way to give me what I really want." Like the wedding.

We opened the rest of the packages. Rachel and Alan received more traditional gifts, while the same people got Art and me more adventurous things. The Reynolds siblings and their partners gave us a weekend getaway at one of the five star resorts on the shore of Lake Michigan. They'd attached the certificate to a bottle of Eli's new wine. I expected most of the shopkeepers on the Square gave us gift cards by the number of cards Rachel had given Art.

I'll always remember the gift that Alan, Rachel, and Thomas gave us. Thomas stood next to me while I unwrapped it. They'd fashioned a huge heart from construction paper and put pictures of the five of us in a circle within the heart. Underneath the heart was printed *My Family.*

"See, Nana. That's me and you and Mom and Alan and Art. We're all married together," Thomas said.

A few tears pooled in my eyes. "Yes, we are, Thomas, yes, we are. Isn't it wonderful?" I gathered Thomas in my arms and gave him a big hug.

I set the picture aside and walked over to the front window to look out over Wolf Creek Square. The white lights were shining brightly in the late afternoon darkness. Art came up behind me and wrapped me in arms filled with love.

It was time for us to go home.

Acknowledgements

I would like to give a special thank you to all the readers, along with family and friends, who made it clear they wanted to read more about shopkeepers and residents of Wolf Creek Square. As one reader said, "Keep on keeping on. I'm waiting for the next book." That's the magic sentence every author wants to hear! What a wonderful gift.

Above all others, I'd like to thank my husband, Gary, for the encouragement and support he gives me. Life is never dull in our house.

A shout out to special writer friends that have been on this journey with me: Kate Bowman, Shirley Cayer, Virginia McCullough, and Barbara Raffin.

To members of the Romance Writers of America, my friends in the Greater Green Bay Area of the Wisconsin chapter and all the individuals associated with these organizations, thank you.

To Brittiany Koren and the Written Dreams team, for considering the last book in the series as important as the first. I thank you.

Gini Athey
2018

About the Author

Gini Athey grew up in a house of readers, so much so it wasn't unusual for members of her family to sit around the table and read while they were eating. But early on, she showed limited interest in the pastime. In fact, on one trip to the library to pick out a book for a school book report, she recalls telling the librarian, "I want books with thick pages and big print."

Eventually that all changed. Today Gini usually reads three or four books at the same time, and her to-be-read pile towers next to a favorite chair. She reads widely in many genres, but her favorite books focus on families, with all their various challenges and rewards.

For many years, Gini has been a member of the Wisconsin chapter (WisRWA) of the Romance Writers of America and has served in a variety of administrative positions.

Avid travelers, Gini and her husband live in a rural area west of Green Bay, Wisconsin.

Silver Bells, a bonus novella, is the seventh story in her Wolf Creek Square series.

Made in United States
North Haven, CT
06 July 2022

20976195R10082